CS THOMPSON

WHY BRISTOL?
MURDER AT BMS

A FOURTH NATASHA McMORALES MYSTERY

Published in the U.S. by:
James One Institute
Bristol, TN

Csthompsonbooks.com

ISBN: 978-0-9794116-8-7

Acknowledgments

A special thanks to those who made major editorial contributions (and corrections to my limited writing skills): Anne Southerland, Bob Land, Craig McDonald, and Sarah Barker.

For technical support and contributions/suggestions to the plot, settings, places, and my word choices: Andria Meade, Barb Thompson, Benny Barry, Brandon Story, Caudell Williams, David Rowe, Dyan Buck, Erin Reardon, Esther Kerr, and Mary Massarueh.

To the folks at Cumberland Marketing: Drew, Jean, Joseph, & Kevin.

To Carol and Gary Rosenberg at The Book Couple.

And to all those folks who let me use their real names in fictitious ways: Amanda Darnell White, Cami Timmons Armbrust, Carol Watson, Corey Henson, Jackie Ke, Justin "Dok" Doktor, Kent Paulette, Mac McElroy, Maggie Lawson, Michael Wade, Pam Zalewski, Robin Bailey, and Roscoe "Sorceo" Phillips.

Prologue

"WHERE ARE THE MIKE & IKES?" groaned Angie as she stood up and stretched. Her back was still tender from her pregnancy three months earlier, and she had just placed six daisies in the brass urn at the base of her father's headstone.

It had been four years since Ike Simmons died. The cancer that took him worked quickly. A wife, Michelle, and a daughter named Angie survived him. Every August 15, Ike's birthday, Angie drove her mother to Ike's gravesite, where they each left a gift of remembrance. Angie always left a bouquet of six flowers. So when her mother called her the night before to say she needed to go to the gravesite at West Memorial Park Cemetery today, Angie cut six daisies from her garden. It was what she always did for his birthday, so even though it was only May 3, she did it today.

Michelle's gift of remembrance was different. On Ike's birthday she would scatter the contents of a box of Mike & Ikes candy around his grave. It was not just that Mike & Ikes were his favorite candy, but ever since she began dating Ike in high school her given name of Michelle had been morphed into Mike. They were Mike & Ike. Their high school yearbook designated them the "sweetest couple."

"It's not his birthday, Angie," said Mike.

"I know it isn't his birthday, but Mom, you always bring Mike & Ike's."

Mike sat in her wheelchair with her hands folded across the top of her purse. She did not look at her daughter. She simply stared at the gravestone. "Could I have a few minutes with your father, honey?"

"Sure, Mom." She squatted down and put her arm around her mother's shoulders. "I'll go over there and sit under that tree."

"Thanks, honey."

"Are you okay?"

Mike patted her daughter's arm. "I am. I just have to honor a promise I made to Ike."

Angie stood up and walked over to the bench under the little shade tree. She sat in the shade and surveyed the cemetery. Being early May it was much greener than when they usually came in August. It was also much cooler.

She enjoyed the peacefulness and tried not to look at her mother, but every minute or so she would peek in spite of herself. She could not help it. Up until that very moment she would have said her mother was the most predictable person on earth. Monday was laundry and fish sticks. Tuesday was knitting and chicken pot pie. Today was a mystery.

After several minutes she gave up the charade and openly watched her mother. Mike would not know whether she was watching or not as Angie was sitting directly behind her.

Mike's head moved sporadically, as if she were still talking. Whatever she had to say was taking considerably more time than Angie had ever seen her parents converse when they were alive.

As she sat lost in her thoughts over her mother's peculiar behavior, Angie did not notice Mike begin to roll her chair forward toward the headstone. When the sight of her mother struggling to move her wheelchair finally registered with her, Angie jumped up and began to jog. She reached the graveside as her mother was leaning over the left side of her wheelchair.

"What are you doing?" blurted Angie.

In Mike's left hand was a rolled-up newspaper. She was trying to place it in the brass urn alongside Angie's flowers. The urn was just out of her reach, and the paper fell from her hand. Mike sat back in her chair in a huff.

Picking up the paper Angie walked around the chair to face her mother squarely. "I'm serious, Mother. I want to know what this is about. Tell me, or I'm going to take you home."

"That's fine," said Mike. "I'm ready to go. We need to go by the post office first." She withdrew a package from her purse. "I have to mail this for your father."

Angie shook the rolled-up newspaper at Mike like she was scolding a child with her finger. "What's going on, Mom? What is it that you had to wait for four years after Dad died to do?"

Pointing at the paper, she said, "I had to wait for that dip-wad to die."

"Dip-wad," she repeated in a higher octave than her mother's utterance. Her mother's predictability factor was fading faster and faster. In thirty-two years of life she had never heard her mother speak ill of anyone. She unrolled the paper and scanned the page of obituaries until she found the one circled in pencil, "Is that Uncle Dobbie?"

CHAPTER 1

Sunday Lunch at the O'Brien's

IT WAS THE SUNDAY AFTER THE MARCH RACE. In other parts of the world that could mean a marathon or a triathlon or even a dogsled race, but in Bristol, Tennessee, the March race was NASCAR at the Bristol Motor Speedway, BMS. Although Nattie was hardly a NASCAR fan, she, like many Bristolians, cashed in on the race by renting her home out to race fans. For her the race meant some easy extra income and a weekend in her old room at the O'Brien homestead in Johnson City.

The weekend had gone smoothly, even enjoyably. Friday night was a Cary Grant film festival on the Turner Classic Movie channel, and Saturday was spent in Asheville, North Carolina. Sunday meant church and Sunday school, followed by a replay of one of the two over the dinner table.

Except for Trevor, the whole family was in attendance, each in their assigned places. Lionel, the patriarch, at the head of the table, was dressed in a beige linen suit, starched white shirt, and navy blue bow tie, which was still tied tightly around his neck. Across from him sat Ingrid, Nattie's mother, who looked much cooler in her floral summer dress. In her mid-fifties she occasionally highlighted her auburn hair, but that was her only concession to age. The crow's feet around her eyes were the only indicators that she was not the same age as her daughter.

Nattie and Kevin, Ingrid's children from her first marriage, sat on the side of the table to Ingrid's left. Nattie had already changed from her church dress into a nice pair of jeans and a light blue blouse. Her younger brother, Kevin, ever the one to stray beyond the family norms, had worn shorts and a short-sleeved, pink, pinstriped oxford shirt, which was not tucked in. His shift into his lunch attire was to remove the shirt. *At least his white T-shirt is clean,* mused Nattie to herself.

Across the table from Ingrid's kids sat Samantha, Lionel's daughter from his first marriage. She was chronologically three years older than Nattie, but at a distance most would have guessed she was the eldest of the three women at the table. Samantha's church attire included a matching brown skirt and jacket, with a white blouse buttoned all the way to the throat. Her uniform made no allowance for the March weather. Samantha's husband, Elijah Gorzilanski, a lawyer at Lionel's law firm, had removed his tie and jacket, and rolled up the sleeves of his white shirt. The empty chair between them would have been Trevor's had he not been invited to a friend's house after church. Elijah sat with his arm around the empty chair. *Without Trevor to distract you time is going to move much slower today, Elijah,* predicted Nattie.

Today the lucky winner for the replay was the Sunday school lesson, which was out of the Old Testament. Nattie had hoped it would be the sermon on Second Timothy, as it was fresh and provocative. The preacher said that sometimes the people who look religious are really self-promoting hypocrites who should be avoided. Nattie wanted to ask how to tell who was real and who was not, but it was not to be.

"Dagon," blurted Kevin, "isn't that the god from *Conan the Destroyer?*"

"*Conan the Destroyer,*" repeated Samantha. "What is that, one of your comic books?"

"It's not a comic book. It's a movie. It's the sequel to *Conan the Barbarian.*"

"There's a sequel already?" The elevation in pitch at the end of Ingrid's question communicated her disapproval.

"Not that Conan movie, Mom, the original one with Arnold Schwarzenegger. The one in the theaters now is a remake."

"Have you seen the new one?" asked Eli, which brought an immediate glare from Samantha.

"Oh yeah, I saw it last week."

"What would you say is the main attraction of that movie—the acting or the plot?"

Ignoring his mother's question Kevin offered, "As a matter of fact it was disappointing. I thought the Schwarzenegger version was better."

"Now there's a phrase I never expected to hear," said Nattie.

Nattie's comment drew an uncharacteristic raucous laugh from Lionel at his place at the head of the table.

Blank open-mouthed stares watched him from around the table. He could not have attracted more attention if he had burst into flames.

"Lionel, honey," said Ingrid from the other end of the table, her voice subdued. "Are you alright?"

Lionel nodded that he was but could not catch his breath to speak. He removed his glasses and wiped his eyes with the handkerchief he carried in his back pocket.

"It's just that I haven't thought about that movie for a long time."

"Wait a minute," demanded Samantha, pressing both palms on the table in an effort to stop time. "Are you telling us that you went to see that movie?"

"Alright. Way to go, O.B.!" O.B., short for O'Brien, was Kevin's term of endearment for his stepfather. Lionel had never heard it before.

Lionel never heard Kevin call him O.B. this time either, as his attention was focused on Samantha. "Why do you ask, Sam? Am I such

6

an old fuddy-duddy that you can't picture me going to a movie like that?"

Only a fuddy-duddy would use the term "fuddy-duddy," thought Nattie. Samantha did not answer.

"It was at least thirty years ago. You were a baby," he said, tipping his head toward Samantha. "It was right after I finished law school, and we were living in Charlotte at the time. I was a volunteer on the Young Life staff working with high school kids, and a couple of guys asked me to go to the movie with them. Of course I said yes."

"How was it?" Ingrid asked the question that was on everyone's mind.

"Blood and guts. Muscle-bound brutes in hand-to-hand combat. It was your typical action movie for regular teenage boys." He paused and looked at the empty seat between Samantha and Eli. It was where Trevor would be sitting if he had not been invited to a friend's house after church.

Nattie was sure that had Trevor been there, Lionel would not have finished his story. As it was, she was still shocked he did.

"There was one scene that if I had known it was there I would never have agreed to go."

"Tell us," blurted Kevin.

Lionel's face contorted again as he reminded himself of what had brought tears to his eyes a few minutes earlier. Taking a deep breath he began, "Conan had just gotten his freedom and he was running across the wasteland and he came to this cave where a beautiful woman lived and of course she seduced him. And in the middle of their —" his eyes searched the ceiling for a word—"ecstasy, the seductress turned into a demon with cat eyes and razor-sharp teeth."

"I remember that," Kevin said, offering his support and encouragement.

"As I watched, all I could think about was, *What are their parents going to think, and what is the Young Life director going to do?* I was mortified, and then Conan threw her into the fireplace where she turned into a ball of flame and flew around the room laughing." He grinned, "And that's when the kid sitting next to me leaned over and asked, 'Was it like that for you the first time?'"

The conversation came to a stop once more as Lionel teared up with laughter again. While everyone else watched Lionel enjoy himself, Nattie stole a glance at her mother. She wanted Ingrid to ask him, "Well, was it?" but she would never have said so out loud. To her amazement Ingrid was returning her glance. When their eyes locked together Ingrid furrowed her brow as if to say, "Behave yourself, I know what you are thinking." *But she couldn't know, could she?*

"What were we talking about?" asked Lionel when he regained his composure.

"Conan." Kevin was the first to answer.

Samantha followed, "We were talking about the passage from the book of First Samuel." Glaring at Kevin she added, "That's what we studied this morning in Sunday school."

"Perhaps you could catch Kevin up to speed about that passage before we get back to your question, Sam."

She frowned at her father, but turning toward Kevin she obeyed his request. "Israel was at war with the Philistines, and they captured the Ark of the Covenant and took it. Do you know what the Ark of the Covenant is, Kevin?"

"Oh sure. I saw *Indiana Jones and the Raiders of the Lost Ark.*" He turned toward Lionel. "That's the Ark, right?"

Lionel bobbed his head back and forth looking for words. "It is what they were referring to, but it was hardly an accurate portrayal of the Ark. Please continue, Sam."

"The Philistines worshiped a statue named Dagon." She immediately held her palm out toward Kevin, cutting off what she anticipated from him. "That's the name of the god from your conehead movie, and this is probably where they got it."

Grinning, Kevin quickly glanced around the table hoping to make eye contact with someone else who heard her mispronounce "Conan." No one returned his look.

"The first night the Philistines had the Ark, they put it next the statue of their god, Dagon, and the next morning it was on its face."

"The statue was on its face?"

"Yes, Kevin, the statue was on its face," she replied without looking at him. "So they stood him back up, and the next morning when they returned he was face down again with his head and arms broken off."

"That'll show 'em." The comment earned Kevin more dirty looks from his mother and Samantha.

"Well, what was wrong with saying that?" he asked.

"It's not that it was so wrong, Kevin," answered his mother. "It's just that you were being . . ."

"It's just that you were being you," interjected Samantha.

"Now, Samantha," Lionel said in the low and slow voice he used to indicate he was about to be insightful, "Kevin was right. That was a display that should have shown them who God is."

"It should have," repeated Kevin. "Do you mean they went back to worshipping that statue? Even though it had no head?"

Maintaining his low and slow voice Lionel answered, "I believe they did."

"That's incredible," observed Kevin.

"It is incredible," agreed Ingrid. "Why didn't they recognize the true God?"

"Yes, that's my question, too," piped in Samantha.

"That's a good question to chew on after lunch," agreed Lionel. Then after a brief scan around the table he focused on Samantha's husband, who was sitting to his right. "How about you, Eli?"

Upon hearing his name Eli came back from whatever cerebral place he had gone. "Excuse me?"

"He wants to know why you think the Philistines didn't accept the God of Israel, Eli," explained Samantha in a nasally voice.

"Yeah, especially after the God of Israel broke the head off their god," added Kevin.

"I suppose they didn't want to stop doing what they were doing."

Kevin laughed. "And the moral of the story is that if you are going to do something your god doesn't approve of, it is better to knock his head off first."

"Kevin!" scolded Ingrid.

"Seriously," Kevin continued, "how would he know what you were doing without a head?"

"Stop that right now," demanded Ingrid.

"I think he's right, Ingrid."

Lionel's defense of Kevin halted all discussion. Everyone, including Kevin, looked at him in disbelief.

"He wasn't being disrespectful to God. He was making fun of Dagon and the people who would worship a god who could get his head knocked off. Right, Kevin?"

"Right O.B."

Nattie and her mother shared another knowing glance. *Is Kevin becoming the prodigal son?* was Nattie's unspoken question. She only guessed that her mother was wondering the same thing. And then another thought hit her: *If Kevin is becoming the prodigal son, then what does that make Samantha?* This unspoken question shifted her attention to her stepsister across the table.

Samantha had been watching the silent mother-daughter exchange but looked away when Nattie turned toward her.

Were you glaring at us? wondered Nattie. Samantha's disapproving glares had haunted Nattie during the early part of her adolescence when she was a new eighth-grader who hadn't figured out how to fit in and Samantha was a senior on the church youth group leadership team.

"How about you, Samantha?" asked Lionel, who had missed all the action at the female end of the table. "What do you think kept the Philistines from accepting the God of Israel?"

"Pride," she said immediately.

Nattie rolled her eyes involuntarily. To her, Samantha's answer denouncing pride sounded a touch arrogant.

"What was that?" demanded Samantha tersely.

Nattie was startled by the question and by the tone in which it was asked. She was startled even more when, upon looking at Samantha, she realized the question was aimed at her. "What was what?"

"You rolled your eyes. Was there something wrong with my answer?"

Nattie took a deep breath. Her instinct was to apologize immediately and try to explain it away without further ruffling her sister's feathers. But she was learning that what she had always considered instinctive compassion was really the conditioned reflexes of the caretaker role she had adopted in her alcoholic family. Charlotte, her therapist, had encouraged her to catch herself at such moments and speak truthfully—"the truth tempered with love" was Charlotte's phrase.

"I am not aware of rolling my eyes, but if you say I did, then I am sure I did. I am sorry if that hurt you."

"Well, why would you roll your eyes at that anyway?"

Another deep breath. Another reminder, *The truth tempered with love.* "Since you have asked me, Samantha, you deserve to hear the answer. When I hear church people use the word 'pride' to explain every human frailty and sin, it makes me flinch. I'm sure the word has its place, but it is a discussion killer."

" 'Discussion killer'?" asked Lionel.

"Yes. Like when someone asks what's your favorite book and as soon as anyone says 'the Bible,' that's the answer everyone else must give."

"But it may be true," countered Samantha.

"True or not, it is an automatic response given without thought. It is expected and it is given because it is expected, not because it is true."

"That was a bit harsh, Nattie," observed Ingrid.

Nattie and her mother locked eyes again for a moment before Nattie turned to Samantha. "I apologize for my harshness, Samantha. I'm new at saying what I really think. I'm sure I don't do it well."

"I think she's right," declared Eli.

"You think she's right about what?"

Eli answered Samantha's question without looking at her. "I think we overuse the pride explanation."

After he spoke he turned to her and mouthed, "I'm sorry." Then he put his hand on the table near hers.

Samantha rolled her hand toward his, and when he stroked the back of it, she looked at him and smiled.

Given enough time Nattie may have felt guilty for watching such a tender, private moment, but before it registered on her, Lionel asked, "Do you have a better explanation for the Philistines' refusal to accept the God of Israel, Nattie?"

"I do," offered Kevin.

Thank you, Kev, thought Nattie, as she said, "Go for it."

"You keep using the phrase 'the God of Israel,' right?" He did not wait for an answer. "So if the Philistines knew he is the God of Israel, then even though they knew he was stronger than Dagon, they may not have trusted he would be their God."

The table was speechless again. Kevin's theological insight was the most recent of the uncharacteristic utterances that had come from four of the six people around the table. Besides Kevin's theological insight, Nattie told the truth, Lionel told a joke, and Eli told Samantha she was wrong. It was a banner day at the O'Brien household, and as soon as Nattie said as much to herself, her cell phone began to vibrate.

With a margin of expectation that it would be Nathan, she looked at the face of her iPhone. The call was from an Amanda White. Nattie did not recognize the name, so she left her to leave a message.

"That's very insightful, Kevin," said Lionel.

"Yes, it was," contributed Eli.

Ingrid nodded her agreement.

Not to be out done by the prodigal, Samantha put her own spin on it. "I agree, there would be no assurance that God's love would extend beyond Israel for another thousand years."

Oh great, thought Nattie, trying hard not to roll her eyes again. *If you all keep this up, Kevin will be even more impossible to live with than he usually is.*

"Have you been doing some Bible study on your own?" asked Lionel.

Nattie's phone vibrated again. It was Amanda White again. *I don't know who you are Amanda, but thank you for giving me a way out of the Kevin Johnson fan club.* "I'm sorry," she said, standing up. "I have to take this call."

No one seemed to notice her exit.

"Hello."

"Nattie?" The voice was not familiar.

"Yes."

"This is Amanda Darnell White from your yoga class."

"Hello, Amanda. What can I do for you?"

"I got your name and number from Maggie Lawson."

"Maggie Lawson, Miss Virginia from last year?" Nattie had worked security during the pageant. For obvious reasons they had wanted a female to be on duty in the changing room where evening gowns were shed and swimsuits were adjusted. Nattie remembered her because of a conversation about Maggie's psychology major, which is what Nattie wanted to major in before she left school. Nattie was glad Maggie won.

"Miss Virginia Teen USA," corrected Amanda. "She said you were a very good detective and were trustworthy and discreet."

"I'm glad to hear that. Are you in need of a discreet detective?"

"You probably didn't know, but I work over at the Speedway."

"I didn't know that."

"Well, I do."

Nattie waited, aware that eventually Amanda would answer her question.

Amanda's voice got softer. Nattie wondered if someone near her might be listening. "Can you come by the track first thing tomorrow morning and discuss something delicate?"

It meant changing her standing Monday morning breakfast with Debbie Duncan. "Sure."

"Aren't you curious about what this is?"

"Of course I am, but it sounded to me like you couldn't talk about it, so I can wait until tomorrow. That's true, isn't it?"

"Yes," her voice was still muted.

"Well, I will see you tomorrow morning then."

"Thank you."

"Where's Kevin?" asked Nattie as she reentered the dining room, finding her brother's seat empty. Between the phone call and a trip to the bathroom she had only been gone a few minutes.

Samantha explained, "He said he had to obey Judges 9:21 and left."

"Can you believe that? He quoted from the Old Testament." Ingrid beamed.

"Technically he didn't quote it, he just referenced it." Samantha was fitting nicely into the role of the prodigal son's older sibling.

I smell something fishy, Nattie thought. She knew there was no telling what obscure piece of information Kevin might store away in his mind, but there was also no telling what his reason would be for doing so. "Does anyone know what that passage says?"

After a moment without a volunteer Lionel turned to Nattie, who was still standing. Pointing at the sideboard he asked, "Nattie, would you mind handing me my Bible from over there, please? We can just look it up."

"Judges 9:21," he repeated slowly while thumbing through the pages. When he came to the passage he read it aloud. "Then Jotham fled, escaping to Bay-ear, and he lived there because he was afraid of his brother Abimelech."

"Did he leave because he's afraid of one of his siblings?" asked Eli with a grin.

"You're the brother-in-law," Samantha slapped his arm playfully. "What about that town? Is there anything special about it?"

"Bay-ear," repeated Lionel.

Nattie bent down close enough to read the passage over Lionel's shoulder. *That's it,* she realized as she read the words herself. The name of the town Lionel pronounced as Bay-ear was actually spelled "Beer." Jotham had gone to "beer," and so had Kevin.

CHAPTER 2

Pam Zalewski

AMANDA'S DIRECTIONS TO THE BRISTOL MOTOR SPEEDWAY had seemed simple enough when Nattie printed her email that morning: "Use the North Entrance next to the giant marquee and come to the white building on the hill next to the Speedway. When you come in the double doors you will see Pam Zalewski sitting in a window. Tell her that you are here to see me, and I'll come get you." But it took her a while to find the hill. Had she looked for it driving by, she would have seen it immediately, but from the middle of the deserted parking lot where she sat, all she could see was a one-story white building in a gully to her left and what she thought was an embankment to her right.

Nattie knew she was missing something, and it frustrated her. She found reading instructions equally as difficult as she found reading people easy. *There's no hill here and no white building,* she thought as she looked at a stone embankment to her right. She considered calling Amanda but fought it off because she suspected she was missing something obvious. As she stared at the embankment, another car entered the parking lot and drove directly for it. *It's a ramp, you knucklehead,* she chided herself, watching the car climb up the incline.

A minute later Nattie parked her car across from the white building on top of the hill. Burton Smith's name adorned the front entrance. She entered through the glass doors and walked to the middle of what looked like a two-story, plantless atrium. A large, brightly lit gift shop took up the entire left wall. Across from the gift shop was a series of ticket windows.

Stepping up to one of the ticket windows she said, "Pam Zalewski?"

The slender blonde behind the window looked up from the counter. She was listening to someone on a Bluetooth in her right ear. "Around the corner," she mouthed, pointing to her left.

Around the corner from the ticket window was a small hallway leading to a double door. A middle-aged woman sat in a built-in booth along the left side of that little hallway. The nameplate on the counter confirmed that this was Pam Zalewski. A small picture frame sitting next to the nameplate framed a calligraphy print. Since Pam was tending to a phone call, Nattie picked up the print and read it. "A woman is like a teabag—you never know how strong she is until you put her in hot water."

"Are we in hot water?"

The voice was soft and sweet, almost timid, but it startled Nattie nonetheless. "I'm sorry."

"You're the detective, aren't you?" asked Pam.

Handing her a business card, "I'm Nattie Moreland, and yes, I am a private investigator. I'm here to see Amanda Darnell White."

After examining the business card Pam picked up the phone, pushed a button, and told someone, "Detective McMorales is here."

"I'm not really Natasha McMorales," explained Nattie. "It's the name of the agency. Like I said, I'm Nattie Moreland."

"I'm sorry," said Pam. "I can call back and tell them Nattie Moreland is here if that's what you prefer."

"Thank you, Pam, but that's okay. I usually have to explain that everywhere I go," said Nattie, adding, "You are Pam Zalewski, aren't you?"

Smiling, the response came, "Yes, dear. Miss White will be down to get you in a moment."

Extending her hand, Nattie said, "Thanks, Pam."

Pam's grip was gentle. "Are we in hot water?" she asked again.

"I'm not sure, Pam." It was the truth. The call from Amanda had not included any details. "I'll know more after my meeting upstairs. Do you know what it's about?"

Pam's eyes got a bit wider. "All I know is that something bad happened across the street after the race Saturday night. I think it was one of the gypsies."

"Gypsies?"

"I'm sorry, that's probably not a nice term. The official NASCAR vendors all have big NASCAR rigs, and they set up on this side of the street. They follow the NASCAR circuit with the racers. The vendors on the other side of the street are different. They're the ones who come here for races, but after the race they'll go to county fairs around here instead of following the race."

"I see."

"Mr. McElroy—he's the general manager—came in Sunday afternoon and the whole public relations department came in, too. So whatever it was that happened has got them pretty shook up."

Nattie had to lean across the counter to hear as Pam's voice got soft. "How did you hear about the Sunday meeting?"

Instead of answering, Pam scrunched her face up and quickly looked toward the double door.

Slow down, Nattie told herself, *you hit a nerve.* Changing the subject she picked up the print. "I love this teabag quote."

Pam's relaxed smile began to return. "Me, too. My sister made that for me. It was a favorite expression of my mother's."

Curiosity about what hot water Pam's mother had been in crossed through Nattie's awareness, but she said, "It's a great quote. "

"Thank you."

"So, Pam, I take it there's a decent grapevine here."

Pam looked directly at Nattie.

"Is the grapevine worried about hot water?"

Pam nodded.

"What does the grapevine say about what happened Saturday night?"

"I heard someone got killed bad."

" 'Killed bad'? What does that mean?"

With widening eyes Pam shook her head rapidly.

"Who?" "Where?" and "How?" were questions Nattie would have to ask later, as Amanda Darnell White opened the double doors to the inner offices.

"Come on in, Natalie," waved Amanda as she held the door open by bracing her back against it. She nodded for Nattie to hurry, which might have meant she was anxious for their meeting to begin. It may have also meant she was losing her battle with the door.

As Nattie stepped through, she glanced back over her shoulder at Pam, who was still watching her wide-eyed. Just before the door closed, she mouthed, "Killed bad."

CHAPTER 3

Amanda Darnell White

ONCE THE DOOR WAS COMPLETELY SHUT, Amanda stepped close to Nattie. In a low voice she said, "We're going upstairs to the conference room."

"Okay." The statement seemed odd. Of course they were going to a conference room.

Amanda turned toward the elevator but hesitated.

"Amanda, are you okay?"

She turned back to face Nattie. She had the same wide-eyed look that Pam Zalewski had. "They're waiting upstairs."

"Who's waiting upstairs?"

"My boss, Emma Iverson, and her boss, Mac McElroy. There's just a lot of tension right now."

"Tension about the murder?" asked Nattie.

"Well, not just that. We decided to print tickets without prices this year, and that made a lot of our season ticket holders angry. And then there's the change we made to the track. I'm sure you've heard about that."

Flinching apologetically Nattie answered, "I'm afraid not. I don't even know who won this year."

"Brad Keselowski won. It's his second win here. He drives the Miller Lite car. Matt Kenseth came in second."

"And did the changes to the track effect the outcome?"

"I don't know," answered Amanda. "It made the surface less slick."

"So less accidents," stated Nattie.

"It's supposed to make it safer to race here, but some of the fans think it takes away some of the skill, too." Then, suddenly, "I think they're having second thoughts," blurted Amanda sheepishly.

"Second thoughts about me?"

Tightening her lips, Amanda responded, "Yes, I'm sorry. Calling you was my idea."

"Are we still going to meet with them, or did they send you down here to send me away?"

The answer was preceded by a sigh. "The meeting is still on."

"But they aren't going to hire me."

"I'm sorry."

Nattie stepped forward alongside Amanda and rested her hand on Amanda's shoulder. "Look, Amanda, if you are worried about me, then please let it go. If I don't get this job, then I don't get this job. It isn't your fault one way or the other."

Amanda smiled.

"I appreciate that you thought of me."

"I just wish it had worked out."

"It still might." Amanda's head pulled back.

Nattie laughed. "I mean, it is nice to know the job is already lost. That takes all the pressure off. I'll just go in there and take my best shot."

"That's an interesting way to look at it."

"Well," Nattie flipped her hands over, "it's not like I could make a mistake and blow it."

Amanda took a deep breath. "Are you ready?"

"Actually I could use a trip to the ladies' room. Is that possible?"

Nodding her head, Amanda looked around as if she had to remember where the bathrooms were located on the first floor. "Follow me."

Nattie was glad to have the bathroom to herself. She settled into one of the two stalls and took out her cell phone. As she dialed she prayed that John Early was available to talk to her and that he knew something that would help. She estimated she had two or three minutes before raising suspicion.

"Natasha," answered Officer Early.

"Hi, John, this is Nattie. I'm in a jam here and hope you can help."

"If it's something I can do while I'm sitting here across from King College watching this speed gun, then I'd be delighted."

"Can you tell me anything about the murder out at the racetrack this weekend?"

John made a whistling noise. "My goodness, Nattie, are you involved with that?"

"Not yet, but I'm up for it."

"It's gruesome."

"What can you tell me, John? The receptionist here told me someone was 'killed bad,' but I don't know any more than that. Heck, I don't even know what 'killed bad' means."

"Well, I can't tell you what that means at this point. It's not my case, and the means of death are a significant part of the investigation. But I can tell you that it was a male vendor who had been working the race. He was the second vendor to get killed by exactly the same method. The first one happened at the August race last year, and now this one at the next race makes it look a lot like some kind of pattern. Marissa Ferguson is the lead detective. Do you know her?"

"No, I don't."

"Well, she'll work with you if you get the job. I'll help you connect with her."

"Thanks, John. Are there any leads yet?"

"Not that I know of. Like I said, though, both the victims were vendors at the race, but they weren't NASCAR vendors."

"NASCAR vendors?"

"The ones who sell official NASCAR stuff and are set up on the Bristol Motor Speedway property are NASCAR vendors. Other vendors who sell food and other stuff are different. They set up their tents all along Volunteer Parkway."

"Do you know what either of the deceased sold?"

"No, but I do know this: They were both men in their early sixties, and they were both in a group that traveled to carnivals and county fairs together."

"Thanks for the tips, John. I appreciate it."

"No problem. I hope it helps."

"Thanks for that, too."

"And Nattie."

"Yes, John."

"The receptionist was right. They were killed bad."

CHAPTER 4

The Conference Room at BMS

POINTING TO HER LEFT AS SHE EXITED THE ELEVATOR Amanda said, "That's the marketing department down there." Then turning to the right she added, "Public relations and event planning are this way."

Nattie followed as Amanda led her along a walkway that overlooked the first-floor entryway. Nattie looked down and watched the Speedway Gift Shop disappear underneath them as they made their way to the other side of the building.

The conference room was directly above the gift shop. A table surrounded by eight chairs took up most of the room. Two women stood behind the table as they entered the room.

"This is Natalie Moreland, the private investigator from Bristol," stated Amanda with an air of professionalism. No hint remained of the tentative insecurity that she displayed on the first floor.

"Cami Timmons Armbrust," said the woman closest to her. She was a bit younger than Amanda, maybe in her early thirties, average height and weight and a big playful smile that made her eyes narrow. Her skillful handshake matched Nattie's in strength and movement.

Cami stepped back, and the other woman moved forward. "It's very nice to meet you, Ms. Moreland. I'm Emma Iverson. I'm the director of public relations here." Emma was fifteen or twenty years older than Cami, a foot shorter, and wore her dark hair pulled tightly back. Emma's handshake was firm, but instead of pumping up and down, she twisted her hand to the right.

Nattie let go of her hand immediately but noted that Emma looked disappointed. *Was that a power game?* wondered Nattie. *Or was it payback for making you wait for me to come upstairs?* "I'm sorry to make you wait."

"It's okay," offered Cami. "Amanda called up here and told us you were in the bathroom."

"Cami!" scolded Emma.

Cami laughed. "I'm the crude one," she confessed without looking at her boss.

"Miss Moreland, if you would be so kind as to take a seat." Emma pointed at the middle chair with its back to the glass wall. "And Miss Timmons Armbrust, would you please go tell Mr. McElroy that we are ready to begin?"

Cami pulled the chair at the left back corner out from the table. "Oh, Mac knows she's here. He'll be here in a minute." She never took her eyes off of Nattie as she dropped into her seat. "Sit down, sit down," she urged.

Amanda took the seat at the left end of the table next to Cami. To Nattie, the women looked like three sisters. The bubbly Cami had the role of the youngest—playful, coy, and pampered. Emma was clearly in the role of the oldest child—conservative, formal, and responsible. Amanda, the middle child, seemed caught in an unstable place between Emma's fondness for protocol and Cami's disregard of it.

"Miss Moreland," began Emma as Nattie took her seat. She stood behind the chair directly across from Nattie. "The investigation that you are being considered for is one that requires the utmost discretion."

"We're PR people," chimed in Cami.

Amanda grinned.

"We are public relations people. It is our job, our responsibility, to present the right image to the Speedway's patrons," continued Emma. "Should we decide on hiring your agency, what assurances can you give us that your firm is discreet?"

"That is a difficult question to answer, Ms. Iverson. The Natasha McMorales Detective Agency is small. I do all of the fieldwork personally. My office manager does the computer work and runs the office, but I have complete and absolute control over any and all information that flows through that office. So I can simply say that the discretion of my agency is equal to my personal discretion."

Emma studied her for a moment, then said, "Some people would contend that women talk too much."

"Are the people who say that men?"

Laughing loudly Cami looked over her shoulder at Emma. Amanda laughed also, but kept her eyes on Nattie.

"You said my question was difficult to answer, but you seemed to have no difficulty in answering," observed Emma.

"The reason I thought it was a difficult question to answer is that if you hire me to investigate something, then I'm going to have to make inquiries and possibly ask questions of someone who does not want to answer questions. No private investigator can guarantee discretion in the wake of their inquiries."

"Well said." It was a man's voice. "Didn't you think that was well put, Emma?" Standing in the doorway he waited. When the attention shifted completely to him, he made his entrance into the conference room. He was six-feet-four, with clear blue eyes and fair skin, and dressed like a retirement home director.

"Mac McElroy," he announced as he approached Nattie. "I'm the general manager here."

"This is Nattie Moreland," said Emma, "the private investigator Amanda brought."

"Good to have you here, Nattie. Did you get a tour of the place?"

"I—"

"We didn't give her time for a tour this morning," interrupted Emma.

"That," he said, raising his eyebrows to emphasize his point, "will have to change. You must come back some time and take a tour as our guest."

"Thank you," said Nattie, finally getting to speak.

He sat down at the head of the table. The boyish charm faded into an adult seriousness. "I assume that you have been briefed on our situation."

Emma looked down, as did Amanda. Cami kept her head up but averted her eyes when Nattie looked in her direction. Nattie wondered, *Did they fail to tell me something that he expected them to tell me?* "What I've been told so far is that there was a murder here Saturday night."

"Not here," blurted Amanda. "The murder was across the street."

Nattie bowed her head toward Amanda. "There was a murder across the street on Saturday after the race. I have not been told the method, but I understand that it was gruesome."

The mention of the method was met with a synchronized flinch from around the table.

"The police," continued Nattie, "consider the method a significant clue, as it is the second murder committed here—I mean, across the street—after a race. The method has not been made public. Marissa Ferguson is the lead detective assigned to the case."

"Do you know her?" asked Mac.

"No, sir, I don't, but I understand she is very thorough and very easy to work with. I believe she will be considerate of your concern for discretion." Nattie was not entirely sure that her last assertion was true. She knew she needed to make a case that a local private investigator would make a better liaison with the Bristol Police Department.

"Do you know the method?" asked Nattie.

Mac looked at Emma. Emma looked at Amanda and Cami. Amanda and Cami held their gaze steady at Emma until she looked back at Mac. Mac sighed and looked back at Nattie. The whole sequence happened rapidly, but it seemed painstakingly slow to Nattie, who experienced it as if she was watching a Three Stooges routine.

"We do know the method, but we have been compelled by the police to silence. If we decide to engage your services we will disclose everything we know."

"I see," said Nattie. "So this is an interview?"

Pooching his bottom lip forward, Mac conceded, "I suppose it is an interview."

"Well, is there a question you would like to ask me then?" *Or have you already decided on a different agency?*

"I can see you are a straightforward person," he noted. "I like that. So you want me to get to it?"

He paused and looked to Nattie for a response. Nattie acknowledged his assertion with a smile.

"We are also considering hiring Ward Rau. Have you heard of them?"

"Out of Chicago?" answered Nattie. It was a complete guess. If it was one of the larger detective agencies, there would be offices in several major cities and Chicago was as good a guess as any.

"Yes, that's right, Chicago."

Nattie nodded. "There is no question that a place like the W. R. Agency can bring quite a bit more resources to the table than I can, but a small, local private investigator can move around this area unnoticed."

"True, but staying in this area is not necessarily going to get the job done, Miss Moreland. When the vendors leave here they follow the NASCAR circuit to Charlotte, Florida, and even New York. I'm afraid that a larger firm can orchestrate that kind of travel more efficiently than you."

"That may or may not be true, Mr. McElroy, but it is irrelevant."

"What?" asked Emma.

"I'm sorry," said Mac.

"The vendors who sell the official NASCAR souvenirs are the ones who follow the NASCAR circuit. The vendors from across the street are a completely different group. The two victims are in that group, and they will stay within a hundred miles of their home base."

Mac's face tightened as he tapped on the table. "You are sure about that fact?"

"I am."

"Where do you get your information?" It was Emma.

"I have sources in local law enforcement," she said, even though the information came from Pam Zalewski downstairs. "I know who to ask for information, and they know what they can trust me with. That's what being local can do."

"Anything else?"

"Excuse me?"

"Does your source have any more information?"

Nattie looked around the room. She definitely had their full attention. She was fairly certain that the job was hers to lose. "Besides being murdered the same way, there is another connection between the two victims."

"What connection is that, Miss Moreland?" asked Emma, who had taken over as the lead interviewer.

"I'll tell you the connection if you tell me the method."

"We aren't supposed to say anything about that."

"Unless you hire me," noted Nattie, which had the effect of directing all eyes toward Mac McElroy at the end of the table.

He studied Nattie for a moment and then turned to Emma. "Go ahead and tell her."

Don't smile, Nattie told herself.

"It seems that you are hired, Miss Moreland. I hope you do not disappoint us."

"You will get my best, that's all I can guarantee. Both victims were part of a group of vendors that traveled together, and that is where I will begin my investigation."

Mac stood up abruptly. "Well done, Miss Moreland. I see that we have made the right choice. Good hunting. Mrs. Iverson will be your contact person from here on." Nodding toward the other end of the table, he said, "Ladies." Then he hurried from the room.

"Do you think he was uncomfortable staying for the rest of the meeting?" asked Cami in a higher voice, which Nattie took as sarcasm.

Emma rolled her eyes. "I suppose you want to hear how these two men were murdered now?"

"If you don't mind."

"They both bled to death."

Nattie waited. There was clearly more to tell. Cami watched Emma with a trace of a smile, as if she were enjoying Emma's discomfort, while Amanda's expression was more like a maternal concern. Emma, for her part, kept her eyes on Nattie.

Nattie realized none of them were going to say more without being asked, "Were they cut somehow?"

Cami snorted.

"In a manner of speaking," answered Emma.

"What was cut?"

"Yeah, Emma," chided Cami, "what was cut . . . off?"

Amanda's eyes got wide as Emma's got tight.

"Oh, come on," said Cami. "I'll tell her." Then, looking at Nattie, "Let's just say that if either of these guys had lived, neither one would be able to pee standing up."

CHAPTER 5

Marissa Ferguson

NATTIE WAS TAKEN TO A SMALL CONFERENCE ROOM at the Bristol, Tennessee, police station. The room had no two-way mirror; moreover, it was so small that a card table and two folding chairs crowded the room sufficiently that it could never have been used as an interrogation room. Before she ruled out converted utility closet, the door opened.

Behind her Nattie heard a male voice. "Hey, Dharma."

Turning around to face the door, Nattie saw the woman referred to as Dharma. Between the medium-blonde hair and the long Alice-in-Wonderland neck, the woman was the spitting image of Jenna Elfman, the actress who played Dharma on *Dharma and Greg*. She was dressed in blue jeans, running shoes, and a plaid blouse over a baby-blue T-shirt.

The tall Dharma look-alike stood in the doorway, studying the room before stepping in all the way. "What is this room?" she said, shaking her head in disbelief. Then, turning toward Nattie, "I'm Marissa Ferguson, and I am sorry about this room. I told the desk sergeant to take you to a meeting room, but I don't know what this is. Come on. Let's go somewhere a little more comfortable."

Nattie stood up to follow her, but instead of leading her from the room, Marissa came to stand over Nattie.

"You are Natasha McMorales, aren't you?" asked the much taller woman, standing so close to Nattie that she had to look up to answer.

"No. I mean, yes. No, wait a minute." She held up her hands in surrender. "You may not believe this, but I do know who I am."

"Are you sure?"

Nattie handed Marissa a business card.

"This says you are Natasha McMorales," Marissa read off the card. Then holding it out for Nattie to see, she asked, "Have you looked at it lately?"

Nattie took a deep breath and readied herself to explain once again how her brother had come to give her that professional name while she was in Nashville acquiring her agency license.

"I'm sorry," Marissa said with a huge grin. "I'm just pulling your chain. John Early gave me the whole story when he set up this meeting. He said you would get a kick out of the question."

"He did, did he?"

"He did. And I believed him." She pulled her head back to look Nattie over. "You look like you could hold your own, though."

"Nothing like you can."

Nattie's comment stopped Marissa's march to the hallway. She turned around.

"I think we've met before," explained Nattie. "If I'm not mistaken we were in a psychology class together at Freedom University."

Marissa's face lit up, and the big smile returned to her mouth. Shaking her index finger, "I do remember you. I think the class was Introduction to Christian Counseling. You sat in the back."

As the recollection settled in, Nattie's eyes got big, and pouting she said, "Yes, that was me. And you sat in the front."

"I did."

"And I remember the professor contradicted himself, and you called it on him."

She put her hands on her hips. "I can't believe you remember that.

It's true; sometimes I just say what I think. I stayed after class and apologized, though."

"You did?"

"Yeah, I didn't want to hurt his feelings."

"I don't think you did."

"No, I don't think I did either." She leaned over the top of Nattie again. "He offered me a job in his office. At the counseling center."

Nattie, ever self-conscious about her height, usually found the habit of tall people getting overly close to be insensitive and often considered it a type of power play, but with Marissa it was feeling friendly and personable. "Did you take the job?"

"No, I didn't. That was my last semester there. I transferred over to King College in my sophomore year. They were just starting a cheerleading squad and offered me a scholarship."

"Cheerleading," repeated Nattie.

"Be careful," she mused. "I may be blond and I may be an ex-cheerleader, but remember," she patted the holster on her hip, "I'm a blond with a gun."

Nattie raised her hands. "I don't know any cheerleader jokes, and I have a genetic aversion to telling blond jokes."

"Let's call it a draw then." Marissa's head dropped an inch as her big smile disappeared. "Would you like to get out of here and get a cup of coffee?"

The lower tone did not strike Nattie as somber, but vulnerable instead. "Sure. Where to?"

"If you don't mind a short walk, we can go down to Manna Bagel or even Blackbird Bakery."

CHAPTER 6

Manna Bagel

THE THREE-BLOCK WALK HAD TAKEN MORE of Nattie's breath than she had anticipated, so she was relieved when they arrived at the back entrance to Manna Bagel. The difficulty was that Marissa's legs were not only quite a bit longer then Nattie's, but Marissa also walked at an athletic pace. Lucky for Nattie, Marissa had the habit of engaging everything she passed with a sense of wonder, which meant her focus was elsewhere. As a result, Nattie did not have to use any of her breath to talk.

On Seventh Street in front of the L. C. King building they passed a woman pushing a stroller holding the hand of a little girl with dark pigtails wearing a blue checked dress. "Is that Little Debbie?" Marissa asked the woman.

The woman, who looked to be in her mid-forties, could have been the child's mother or grandmother. "It is," she answered.

"Did you make that yourself?"

The woman's smile was all the answer necessary.

"It's perfect."

"Thank you."

"Isn't it perfect?" Marissa said to Nattie, who was enjoying the moment of standing still.

"It is," Nattie mustered, trying not to sound out of breath.

Marissa squatted down in front of the stroller and said, "You have a great day, sweetheart."

After the little girl blushed and turned away, the woman told them, "She's shy."

"Well, you two girls have a wonderful day," pronounced Marissa, standing up, and they were off again.

It took Nattie three steps to every one of Marissa's. At least it seemed that way to Nattie. Marissa, for her part, was oblivious to her pace or the effect it had on her much smaller companion. They arrived at the back door of Manna Bagel without further conversation.

"Hey, Nattie. Your brother just left." It was a female voice that Nattie recognized, but having just come into the dark hallway from the bright sun, she needed a moment for her eyes to adjust.

"Oh, hi, Carol. It took me a minute to recognize you." The staff at Manna Bagel all tended toward the friendlier end of the spectrum, but Carol was by far the bubbliest. She was unpacking packages from one of the boxes that lined the hallway. As Nattie and Marissa entered, Carol had to stop and get out of the way. With the boxes along the wall, the hallway was too narrow for more than one person at a time.

"Oh, that's okay," she giggled as she stood aside. "Let me get out of the way. Your brother was here most of the morning."

"All morning? Playing chess?"

"Yes."

"Well, thanks for keeping me posted, Carol. He needs a lot of keeping after."

Beaming, Carol replied, "We do what we can. The rest is in God's hands."

"Say, Carol, do you know Detective Ferguson?"

Carol looked up at Marissa, "You look familiar to me. You've been here a few times, but I don't think I have ever waited on you."

Stepping around Nattie, the Bristol detective said, "Call me Marissa."

"You have beautiful eyes," Carol said as they shook hands. Then, blushing, she added, "I mean they are pretty, but more than that your eyes look wondrous. The eyes are the window to the soul, and I think your soul is full of joy." After a short pause she added, "And wisdom, too, I think."

"Why, thank you, Carol. That was a wonderful thing to say to someone you just met. I bet you see a lot of joy."

"I do," admitted Carol.

"Because you spread joy."

Blushing, Carol shook her head. "Oh, I don't know about that."

"What do you think, Nattie?"

"I agree."

Emerging from the alcove she had retreated to, Carol began to playfully shoo them down the hall. "Oh, you two . . . you are going to give me the big head."

As Nattie and Marissa moved toward the front, Marissa got the last word over her shoulder. "Well, if your head gets too big, we'll just take you to New York and enter you in the Macy's Thanksgiving parade."

Nattie needn't have seen nor heard it to know that Carol was back at her work with a big smile on her face.

"Good morning, Natasha. You just missed your brother," said the woman behind the counter. She was pretty close to Nattie's size and height, but with brown hair pulled back in a perfect ponytail.

"Thanks."

"Hi, Margie," said Marissa. "How are you today?"

"It's a good day," she said, smiling. "Do you want your usual?"

"I always get the breakfast wrap," explained Marissa to Nattie. It was a large wheat tortilla with peanut butter, honey, bananas, and granola. "Have you ever had one? I love them."

"I think we have strawberries," said Maggie, knowing that this was how Nattie preferred her wrap.

"Just coffee for me this morning, thanks."

"No Natasha?"

"No, just coffee."

"A Natasha. What's a Natasha?" Marissa asked Maggie.

Winking, Maggie just tipped her head toward Nattie. "I'll let her tell you while I get your orders."

Wide-eyed, Marissa turned to Nattie. "I'm impressed. There's something here named after you."

"It's not really on the menu, but it's an open-faced grilled cheese sandwich with tomato and onion on a jalapeño bagel. It's a variation of their Continental. My brother came up with it."

"It sounds good."

"It is," piped in Maggie, sliding Marissa's wrap across the counter.

CHAPTER 7

Marissa's Story

"I CAN SEE WHY YOU ARE A DETECTIVE," noted Marissa casually.

Where did that come from? "I'm sorry?" Nattie said after taking a moment to replay Marissa's comment in her head.

"It's your eyes, Nattie. You have a nice, kind face and when you listen you give your full attention to whomever is speaking. Even though we've only spoken briefly I knew I had your full attention. I could tell by your eyes."

Nattie forced herself not to smile.

"I bet you would have been a good counselor, too."

"I don't know about how good I would have been, but when I was in college I was planning on going to grad school and becoming a marriage counselor."

"So, what happened?"

Shrugging, "No money after my sophomore year."

"You know you could probably have gotten enough in loans and grants to have finished."

Not if your family had too much money. "I didn't think of that. My plan was to work a few years and go back."

Marissa grinned, guessing, "And you feel in love with detective work."

Nattie replied, chuckling, "Love is a funny word for it. I've been spit at, blamed, and threatened. I've even been knocked out twice."

"And yet, you still have a perfect nose."

Nattie flinched.

"Boy, that's fun to do."

"What?"

"Make you blush. All it takes is a compliment."

"Well," she paused, trying to think of what to say next, "your nose is perfect, too."

They stared at each other as time slowed down. Nattie's retort hung in the air between them. Then simultaneously they laughed. It was an unconstrained, conspicuous laughter, drawing the attention of the other patrons.

"That's the best you've got?" asked Marissa.

"I'm sure I'll think of something better before I go to sleep."

"I hope you'll let me know if it's really good."

"Of course."

"So if it's not a labor of love, what is it?"

"It was just a job. I started out as a receptionist, and then Hiram— it was his detective agency that I worked for—anyway, he used to have me talk to the wives in the waiting room while he was with his client. He thought I had some kind of gift for getting people to talk to me."

Marissa reached out one finger. Tapping the back of Nattie's right hand, which was resting on the table in a loose fist next to her coffee cup, and causing Nattie to stop speaking, she asked, "What do you think?"

"What do you mean?"

"I mean, do you think you have a gift for that?"

Sighing, Nattie answered, "I'm not sure I understand what that means, but in general people do open up to me and tell me things. If

I'm doing something special to make that happen, then I'm clueless about what it is. All I know is I sort of expect it to happen and it often does."

Marissa smiled.

"Does that make it a gift?"

"Not necessarily, but . . . you never know."

"How about you?"

"Well, my story is similar to yours. I wanted to be a social worker. In fact, I was in my second year of grad school up in Philadelphia doing a practicum at a woman's shelter when I decided to go into law enforcement."

Nattie put both her elbows on the edge of the table and leaned forward.

"There it is, Nattie."

"What?"

"You knew there was a story behind what I just said, and—what did you call it?—you expected to hear it, so your whole body told me to keep talking."

Defensively, "Honestly, Marissa, I wasn't trying to manipulate you."

"Oh, I know that. What you did could not have been more natural. If it wasn't natural, then it wouldn't have worked. If I thought you were trying to trick me, then I'd want to withhold whatever you were after, even if I wanted to tell you in the first place. But like most folks, I want to share my story. I just want to make sure I'm safe first." Marissa leaned forward, "You understand that, too, don't you?"

Whatever Carol had seen in Marissa's eyes in the back hallway suddenly became clear to Nattie, too. "Yes. I do."

"So here's my story," began Marissa. "My grandparents—that's my grandparents on my father's side—live in Kingsport. That's where I spent every Christmas since I was a little girl. My mother's parents didn't care about Christmas so much, and neither did my mother, so that's where I went. My grandmother was afraid I wasn't being taught anything about faith, so before bed every night she would sit me down on her lap in the little sitting room where they put up their Christmas tree and tell me Bible stories. My bed was upstairs, so she couldn't put me to bed because of her broken hip that never completely healed. Anyway, after she finished with a Bible story or two, she would send me upstairs. But she knew I was a little scared to go to bed by myself, so we'd just sit there very quietly and look at the angel on the top of the tree. It was this gorgeous glass angel, and all the lights from below it on the tree sparkled up inside and through it. I swear that glass angel was always placed so that it was looking right down on me in my grandmother's lap. It made me feel safe. That's probably because every night, right after she kissed me and sent me upstairs, she'd say, 'Angels are watching.'"

" 'Angels are watching,'" repeated Nattie. "What does that mean?"

"You know," Marissa's eyes twinkled, and she grinned, "I have never realized this before, but I don't know what it means." Laughing, "I just know it made me feel protected. I'm sure she wanted to make sure I didn't feel alone."

"Did it work?"

Smiling and looking off like she was picturing something pleasant, "Yeah, it did." Then she sighed. "There's a real bittersweet side to that story, though."

Nattie held eye contact but said nothing.

"It's actually why I'm a cop now. Do you want to hear it?"

"Absolutely."

"Well, like you I wanted to do mental health work when I was in college. Social work was what I wanted to do. That's probably because of the social worker who worked with me. I thought she was the most together woman I had ever met. Anyway, after I graduated from Freedom University in Kingsport I went to a social work program in Philadelphia. In my second year I did a practicum at a woman's shelter in a suburb."

"Is that like an internship?"

"Yes, only shorter. At least that's the way it was where I went." She drew an imaginary circle on the tabletop with her index finger and the pace of her speech slowed down. "The women who lived there were all from abusive relationships. Most of them had real tough stories." Flexing her jaw she continued, "One night I got to talking with a woman who was afraid of the dark, and I told her the story about my grandmother and the glass angel."

"You told her angels were watching?"

"I did."

"Did it work?"

Continuing to draw circles on the table, Marissa took a long slow breath, "I suppose you could say that it worked—but it didn't work out."

"It didn't work out?"

Marissa's lips thinned out as she pressed them together and a single tear streaked down her left cheek. She made no effort to wipe it away, and when she turned her face squarely toward Nattie her eyes were clear.

Nattie had never seen anyone cry without hiding their face, at least a little. But Marissa cried openly without a trace of embarrassment. Her eyes were not even red.

"Lila," began Marissa again. Then realizing what she had done, she clamped a hand over her mouth. "Oops! I'm not supposed to use her name."

"I won't tell."

"I know you won't. It's just that I know better." She shrugged. "My story about the glass Christmas tree angel worked so well that after lights out, Lila left the shelter. You see, she had her own glass angel, and after hearing my story she decided that she could not live without it. Against all the rules she went back home. I'm sure she thought she knew her husband's routine well enough that she could get in and out of their home without being noticed, but he came home early from a bar and saw her driving away. That's what he told the police. He followed her back to the parking lot next to the shelter, where he demanded she go with him. I'm not sure what happened next, but after Lila refused to go with him, he threatened her with a gun, they struggled, and the gun went off."

She turned her head away toward State Street.

"I finished out the year, but after what happened to Lila my heart just wasn't in it. That summer I went to the academy, and I've been a cop ever since."

"What happened to Lila?"

Another tear retraced the route left by the first. It was quickly followed by a third. "She died two days later. The internal injuries were too severe."

"You know, it's not your fault. What you told her inspired her. It turned out badly, but not because of you."

"I know. But thank you for saying so. No, I don't blame myself for that. But I do have a regret. It's not that it haunts me or anything, but there is something I wish I had said to her. Something I should have said to her."

A siren sounded outside the restaurant. Both women watched through the window as an ambulance headed up State Street toward the hospital.

As the siren faded Nattie turned back to Marissa, who continued to stare out of the window.

"When they loaded Lila on the gurney and began to put her in the ambulance she panicked. She didn't know where that glass angel was. It was lying on the ground. When I handed it to her, she took hold of it and clutched it to her chest like a little girl." Tears streamed down both cheeks. "She was thirty-five years old, but she was such a little girl."

Turning from the window, "She was such a little girl. It would have meant so much to her if I had just said, 'Angels are watching.'"

There was a pause.

"Well, now that we have that settled, what do you say we get down to business?"

Nattie looked down, unaware that she was knitting her eyebrows together.

"What's the matter, Nattie?"

Looking up, "What do you mean?"

"I mean, when I asked you if you wanted to get down to business, you flinched. I just wondered if you had something else on your mind?"

"Yeah," Nattie blurted, pointing at Marissa. "What you just did. Carol was right. You are wise. You read people, like you just read me."

Marissa grinned. "Maybe so. But no more than you do. I noticed that you flinched. You would have noticed that, too."

Before Nattie could speak, Marissa leaned closer. "Now don't go denying it."

There it is again, thought Nattie. "I wasn't going to deny it." Then with a slight smile she added, "I was going to change the subject and ask a question."

"Okay. What were you going to ask?"

"I was aware that Carol was right. You are wise. I have seen wisdom at work in you. What I'm curious about is how did Carol see it just by looking at your eyes?"

Marissa sat back. "I suspect that Carol is a woman of deep faith, and I suspect she sees many things other people do not see."

"But how? Is it a gift or something?"

"Maybe it is. But whether it is or not is secondary to this: She sees things others don't because she looks for them."

CHAPTER 8

Down to Business

"YOU DO KNOW HOW THEY DIED, don't you?"

"I know the cause of death, but I don't know any of the details."

"The short version is this: Both Herman Ellis and Dick Goldman were completely naked and tied to a folding chair when they were found. Other than the wound that killed them, there were no other wounds or any signs of a struggle. The time of death was estimated to be between 11:00 p.m. and midnight. Dick Goldman was last seen at 10:45, and his body was discovered at 12:30. Each man had a piece of duct tape over his mouth. There were no fingerprints. The Ellis murder happened on the last night of the August 2011 race. The next race at BMS was the March one we just passed. The Goldman murder happened on the last night of that race. Herman Ellis had a large dose of the date rape drug Rohypnol in his system."

"And Dick Goldman?"

"He probably did, too. We'll know for sure when the full autopsy report comes in. I'll let you know."

"Thank you."

"Look, Nattie, I've never worked a case with a private investigator before, so I'm not exactly sure how this will go."

"Me either. In the past, when I've worked on an open case with the police, we did not exactly coordinate our efforts or even brainstorm together. The most I've ever experienced is the sharing of information. I just assumed the police were understandably cautious with an ongoing investigation."

"I'm sure some of that is legitimate. I know my lieutenant will ask me if I personally verified every piece of evidence I report. But there is no need to be territorial either. What do you say if we collaborate, at least our thoughts and maybe our efforts, too?" Before getting an answer she asked, "The Bristol Motor Speedway is picking up your expenses, right?"

"Yes."

"Well, one of us needs to get up to Richmond, and I'm guessing you can get that covered faster than I can."

"They gave me a number to call if I needed to leave the area. They prefer to make the arrangements."

"I thought so. Besides, Nattie, I think we're going to work well together."

"That sounds good to me, but I can't help but wonder what your superiors will think."

"That's easy enough to answer right now. I cleared it with my lieutenant this morning."

Their eyes locked for a moment before a crooked smile gradually formed across Marissa's face.

Still grinning, "Okay, Nattie, you caught me. There is a reason I want to collaborate, and it has nothing to do with how well we could work together. I knew I needed to work with you before I met you, but when I said I thought we'd work well together, I meant that."

"Okay. What is it you need? Besides my expense account?"

"This will need further explanation, but the bottom line is this: One of the Dog Pack won't trust me because I'm a cop."

"The Dog Pack?"

"Yes. That's what that group of vendors that work together at the race called themselves. Both the victims were part of the Dog Pack."

Marissa took a small notepad from her back pocket, opened it, and placed it on the table in front of Nattie. "Here's a list of their names and contact information."

Nattie copied the list of names into her moleskin:

Lucas Dobbs

Abraham Applewhite

Lawrence Yarborough

Grey Troutman

Robert Dobbs

Sunny Hill

"And one of them won't trust you because you are a cop?" clarified Nattie.

"Yes."

"And you want me to see if he'll open up to me."

"She."

"I'm sorry?"

"It's a she. Sunny Hill is a she, and I am hoping she'll open up to you."

Turning to a fresh page in her moleskin notebook Nattie said, "Okay, Marissa, I'm ready. Tell me what I need to know."

"I'll just start with the initial investigation. The first thing we try to do is identify eyewitnesses and collect alibis from all the possible suspects. That was not very productive this time. On the night of the Goldman murder the place was in turmoil. The Saturday race had been over for hours, but there were still lots of people around. With the exception of the campers, most of the fans had cleared out by then. The vendors and the race teams were packing up and gradually heading out, too. That was exactly the same for the Ellis murder last year."

"How did the investigation of that one go?"

"Nowhere," answered Marissa. "Until this happened it was labeled as unsolved, possibly random."

"Well, there's clearly nothing random about it now."

"No, there's not," agreed Marissa. "Whoever did this picked a good time for themselves."

"I'll say. Now that brings us to phase two."

"Motive," said Nattie.

"Yes. Motive. Unless this is entirely random, then we're looking for someone with motive and opportunity."

"And the list of people who had opportunity is pretty wide open, right?"

"To tell you the truth, the only person I am sure didn't do it is me," said Marissa without even a brief chuckle.

"It's a start," observed Nattie, "What's next?"

"Standard procedure would be to interview the family, friends, and associates of the deceased. Now for Dick Goldman, he was survived by a wife. No kids. According to his wife, his associates—the Dog Pack—were also his only friends. The wife, a Vietnamese woman, was in Richmond at the time, and her alibi checks out. An in-person interview of her would be good."

"Which means a trip to Richmond."

"Yes. And three of the six surviving members of the Dog Pack live in Richmond, too."

"Are they all suspects?"

"None of them have great alibis. They were all in the area, but they were all busy breaking camp, so any of them could have done it."

Nattie nodded, "I see."

"The other three surviving members are all in Kingsport. Two brothers named Dobbs and the girl, Sunny Hill."

"The one who doesn't trust cops?"

"I'm not sure if any of them trust cops, but she takes it to a whole other level."

"Do you know why?"

"She's part of a culture that goes back a long way in Appalachia. I wouldn't be surprised if there were moonshiners in her family tree."

"Are you serious?"

"Absolutely. There's a code among those people. And not talking to outsiders, especially the government, is rule number one."

"Do they think you are a revenuer?"

"Maybe. All I know is that to them the government protects the haves from the have-nots. So the have-nots are on their own."

"What about justice?"

"They generally think they can handle that without interference."

Raising her eyebrows, Nattie concluded, "So you want me to go do the interfering."

CHAPTER 9

Sunny Hill

"CAN YOU HELP ME?" ASKED NATTIE. Marissa had told her that when the Dog Pack was not at an event, Sunny could usually be found at the Haggle Shop, an antiques mall on Broad Street in Kingsport. Nattie made a point of arriving early in the morning to avoid customers. She had to meander around over twenty other dealers to find Sunny's area.

"What do you need?" responded the girl behind the counter. The question was asked without looking up. She was thirty-something, straight brown hair, with a physique somewhere between slender and athletic. Her voice was weak—not timid weak, but disengaged weak.

When Nattie did not answer she looked up. She had pretty features on her face—high cheekbones, clear blue eyes with a hint of green, a slender chin, and chiseled lips. In spite of the pretty features the first adjective Nattie thought of when she raised her head was "tired."

"Are you Sunny Hill?"

"And who might you be?" Her eyes were fully focused on Nattie, but her voice remained detached.

"My name is Nattie Moreland. I'm a private investigator from Bristol." Handing over a business card, Nattie waited for the seemingly inevitable Natasha question.

No question came, however. The card was taken and placed in a back pocket.

"You here about Mr. Goldman?"

Nodding, "Do you know anything about that?"

"I know he's dead."

"Do you know anything else?"

"I know how he died."

"Does that worry you?"

"Should it?"

Nattie tipped her head to the right. "If you are Sunny Hill, then I'd think it would concern you that two of your business associates died in the same place and in the same way."

"Do you know how they died?"

"I do."

"Then you should know why I ain't worried about dying that way."

Closing her eyes momentarily Nattie tried to reboot herself. "I seem to have gotten off to a bad start with you. Do you mind if I start over?"

Shrugging, "Suit yourself."

Extending her hand, "Hi, I'm Nattie Moreland."

Although her handshake was soft, her hands were well worn and weathered. This woman, whom Nattie took to be Sunny Hill, was used to hard work, and either she was generally suspicious of strangers or she was hiding something. Either way, Nattie knew she would get further if she worked off the general suspiciousness theory.

"You a detective?"

Nattie nodded yes.

"But you ain't with the police?"

"No. I was hired by the racetrack."

She nodded.

"They are afraid those murders will be bad for business."

She curled her lip and shrugged again.

"Surely you could see why they are concerned."

She stared at Nattie through a poker face.

"Look, Sunny," Nattie called her by name, hoping to get a reaction to confirm what she was 90 percent sure of. Seeing no reaction she continued, "I'm guessing you are a bit suspicious of anyone working for the racetrack."

Sunny nodded her head slightly, and her mouth softened.

"I'm guessing that you haven't felt all that protected by them either."

"I don't need nobody protecting me."

"Maybe not, Sunny, but there are people whose job it is to protect you."

"Tell that to Mr. Ellis and Mr. Goldman."

"I understand. But both of those men were part of a group, and that may mean the other members of that group are at risk."

"And the racetrack cares about that, do they?"

"I can't speak for them, but they hired me to speed up the investigation, and that ends up being the same thing."

"Maybe in your world, but not mine."

"If I can figure out who is doing this, we will put a stop to it."

The lack of appreciation on Sunny's face no longer surprised Nattie, but the complete lack of any response at all was baffling. "I'd think you would want to see justice done?"

"I'd rather see the guilty punished and the innocent protected."

"Isn't that the same thing?"

"Is it?"

"I know we just met, Sunny, but I'm getting the impression that you don't trust the police investigation."

Sunny stared at her.

"I don't guess you trust me either, do you?"

Shaking her head no, "You're just looking for someone to blame."

CHAPTER 10

The Grind House

NATTIE WATCHED MARISSA STROLL INTO THE GRIND HOUSE from one of the tables toward the middle of the coffee shop. If it was possible, she looked even more like Dharma than when Nattie first met her. Maybe it was the way her face lit up with squinty eyes and a toothy smile that would have looked goofy on almost anyone else. That was the smile that appeared on her face when she spotted Nattie.

"It's like a sauna in here," she said as she approached the table where Nattie and Kevin sat. "Is it always this warm?"

Corey, the young man from behind the counter, overheard the comment as he walked toward the front of the shop. "I just checked the thermostat, it was set for eighty."

"Did you turn it down?" asked Kevin in a childlike voice.

"Should I?" retorted Corey without missing a beat. "Oh well, too late now." Then turning to Dharma, "Can I get you anything?"

"I just need a coffee to go."

"Do you know what you want?"

"Regular is fine."

"They have two regular coffees, strong and stronger," offered Kevin.

"Cowboy Up and House," clarified Corey.

"I assume the stronger one is the Cowboy Up?" asked Marissa. After seeing Corey nodding yes, she added, "I'll have a large one of those. Make it to go, please."

As Corey left, Kevin stood up next to Marissa. The fact that she was two inches taller than he did nothing to wipe the seventh-grade-boy look from his face. *Gee whiz, Kevin, can't you tell that she can see the way you're looking at her?*

"I'm Marissa," she said, extending her hand.

Oh, don't encourage him. It'll be like feeding a stray cat. "This is my brother, Kevin, Marissa. He's also the office manager."

"Of the Natasha McMorales Detective Agency," finished Marissa. "I understand that name was your idea."

Kevin blushed. He was still holding her hand, and he had still said nothing out loud.

Relax, Kevin, it wasn't a compliment. "Kevin, how about giving Marissa and I a couple of minutes to talk?"

Shaking his head slightly, as if coming out of a trance, "Oh sure," then stepping away from his seat across from Nattie, "Here you go, Marissa, take my seat. I'll get your coffee."

As Marissa sat down, Kevin stood at the end of the table. "How about a muffin? Sometimes they have a chocolate-espresso muffin. Can I get one for you?"

"No, thanks. Just coffee."

He nodded and turned toward the counter.

"I don't care for one either, Kevin," chided Nattie.

He looked back over his shoulder with one of his "I know you caught me, but aren't I cute anyway?" looks.

"He's cute," observed Marissa.

"Cute" is the right word if you mean amusing in a way that that gets old quick.

"When do you leave for Richmond?" asked Marissa.

"Later this morning. I'm going to see Mrs. Goldman around

54

five o'clock tonight, and tomorrow I'm having breakfast with Abe Applewhite."

"Great. You're really on top of this."

"Well, not everything," confessed Nattie.

Marissa nodded knowingly. "You met Sunny Hill then."

"I did. And I think I can say with great confidence that she doesn't trust me any more than she trusted you."

"It was worth a try. Nothing ventured, nothing gained."

"Just for discussion's sake, let me ask you something."

"Sure. What do you want to know?"

"Are you sure her attitude is a lack of trust?"

"It's at least that," said Marissa. "Have you ever heard of omerta?"

"No," answered Nattie.

"It's a Mafia term. It means 'Don't talk outside the family.' That's the unpardonable sin to them, and for Sunny's people it's the same. I thought you might recognize it from the *Godfather* movies."

"I understand the code of silence, but she could still be hiding something."

Tipping her head to the right, Marissa said, "Anything's possible, I suppose, but if she's trying to avoid suspicion, do you really think she'd be so openly hostile?"

"I'd say her hostility was genuine, but that doesn't mean she couldn't be hiding something else behind it."

"True. As far as I'm concerned, everyone is still a suspect."

Marissa's large Cowboy Up coffee appeared at the table. "Is this yours?" asked Robin, whose dark hair, fair skin, and deep red lipstick gave her a 1950's movie star look.

"It is," answered Marissa, "thanks. What do I owe you?"

"Nothing," answered Robin. "Kevin took care of it."

With my account, no doubt, thought Nattie. "Where is my brother?"

Robin moved her eyes toward the back of the coffeehouse where the bathrooms were located and then returned to the front counter.

"Before your brother gets back, let me ask about your trip."

"Okay," said Nattie.

"Are you all set? I mean, is there anything you need from me before you go?"

"Thanks, Marissa, but no. I think I'm in good shape. I have an appointment with Dick Goldman's widow tomorrow afternoon."

"And the other Dog Pack guys?"

"I made contact with Mr. Applewhite, and he assures me that all three of them will meet with me the next morning."

Surprised, "You're meeting with all three of them at the same time?"

"I am," explained Nattie. "I feel like I can get a lot by watching how people react to each other. If I feel like there's a reason to follow up with them individually, I can always make that happen, too. Why? Is there something wrong with doing it that way?"

"No, not really. It just isn't how I was taught." Then, with a frown, she withdrew her phone, and after a quick look she scowled. "I gotta run," she said. "It looks like I'm in trouble with the lieutenant." Picking up her coffee she added, "Good luck in Richmond. And tell your brother thanks for the coffee."

"I will."

Almost as soon as Marissa left, Kevin reappeared from the bathroom. "Where's your friend?"

"She left, Kevin. And it's a good thing, too."

"What do you mean?"

"Do you ever look yourself over before you leave the bathroom?"

Kevin immediately looked down and noticed the scattering of wet spots down his left leg below his zipper. "Ugh, I hate these pants."

CHAPTER 11

Song Lee Goldman

Richmond, VA

"MRS. GOLDMAN?" ASKED NATTIE TENTATIVELY. She had expected to find the Goldman home filled with friends and relatives attending to the grieving widow, but with only a single car in the carport, she was not sure who would be answering the door.

The short Asian woman in the doorway nodded once and stepped to the side, motioning for Nattie to enter. Mrs. Goldman, half a head shorter than Nattie, bowed several times as Nattie walked in and ushered her down the hallway.

"You are Song Lee Goldman, aren't you?" Nattie tried to clarify.

Avoiding eye contact the Asian woman nodded and continued to herd Nattie down the hallway.

They entered a small, dark living room where a dozen boxes were scattered around the room in various states of construction. Half were sealed shut with tape, three were folded shut, and another three were open. One of the open boxes was half full of shoes, another half full of boots, and the last one was full of neatly folded shirts. On the plastic-covered floral couch was a small pile of unfolded shirts.

"You can take these," offered Mrs. Goldman, pointing at the taped boxes. "I will have the others ready before you are finished."

"I think you have me mistaken for someone else, Mrs. Goldman." Handing her the business card she was holding, "My name is Natalie Moreland. I am a private investigator from Bristol, Tennessee. I'm here to ask you a few questions, if you don't mind."

After glancing at the card she looked Nattie up and down. "You aren't from the church?"

"No, ma'am."

"I was expecting someone from the church."

"I understand."

"But you are not from the church."

"No, ma'am."

The woman sighed and scanned her living room.

A wave of guilt passed over Nattie. This woman had lost her husband less than a week ago. She was obviously working hard to settle some of her affairs, and just as obviously she was behind schedule in doing so. If that was not enough, the woman looked very tired. Nattie was just doing her job, and although she knew that it was a job this woman would want done, she still could not help but feel she was intruding.

"I am so sorry. Please forgive my rudeness," the widow said, pointing to another room. "Please join me in the kitchen. We can talk at the table."

"No apology is necessary. I know this is a very stressful time for you. I am sorry for your loss."

Bowing again, "You are kind."

The kitchen was decorated in bright yellow colors with a rooster theme. There were rooster salt and pepper shakers, roosters on the drapes and in the wallpaper, and rooster figurines lining the top of the shelves.

As Nattie sat down at the table Mrs. Goldman asked, "Tea?"

"No, nothing really. I'd just like to ask you a few questions, and then I will leave you alone."

Settling across from Nattie, "What would you like to know?"

"I want to know anything that you can tell me that might help me find out who did this to your husband."

"Dicky was a good man. He worked very hard in his own way. He was loyal to me and loyal to his Dogs."

"The men he was in business with?"

"The men he was in the war with. That is where Dicky and I met."

"Vietnam?"

"Yes. He was a soldier. I lived there."

"I see. Can you think of anyone who would want to hurt him like that?"

"Yes," answered Song Lee without hesitation.

The crispness of the answer surprised Nattie. "I'd like to hear about that if you don't mind talking about it."

"I'm too old to be embarrassed," she said without blinking. "One of his Dogs went to prison for violating a woman many years ago. Dicky said he was not involved, but I know he was. I don't know how or what, but I know it changed him."

"Changed him how?"

"Before that he was easy."

"Easy?"

She looked down to her right and then her left, searching the table-top for another word. "Carefree. Casual. Easygoing. Easy."

"I see."

"He was still that way after, but sometimes he would get moody. Sometimes he would get irritable, too. He was never like that before. It was like something bothered him."

"Guilt?"

"Yes. Like a dragon in his mind that would breathe fire on him for a while."

"Anything else?"

"Like most men he used to make the jokes that would degrade women. Vietnamese men are like that, too. But after this happened no more."

"Like whatever happened went too far, and it wasn't funny anymore."

"Yes." Looking directly at Nattie she added, "A woman understands."

"Do you know the name of the woman?"

Nodding no, "I cannot remember that far ago, but I know it is in Corporal Simmons's log. He kept a record of everything that ever happened. I remember he called it his log, but the other Dogs called it his diary. He is dead now, but I will give you his wife's information."

"Thank you. That will be very helpful."

After retrieving a small address book from the counter, Song Lee wrote the phone number and address of Michelle Simmons on a recipe card.

"How about the name of the man who went to prison?"

"We have not spoken his name in many years, but I remember the Dogs called him Red because of his hair." Standing up she circled around behind Nattie and retrieved a small framed photograph from the wall behind her. She placed the old photograph of a group of men in army fatigues on the table in front of Nattie.

Tapping the only redheaded man in the picture she said, "See, he has red hair."

There were a dozen men in the picture. Five men were kneeling in front, and the other seven were standing in an arc behind them.

"That is my Dicky," Mrs. Goldman said as she tapped the face of the scrawniest-looking man in the group, the man who occupied the center position in the front row. Then pointing to the man on the left end of the top row she added, "And that is the corporal." Then she returned to her seat across from Nattie before adding, "Their names are written on the back."

Nattie flipped the photograph over and took out her moleskin notebook. Red's name was Reed Hill, a name that was not on the list Marissa had given her. As she wrote the name down she asked, "Is Mr. Hill by any chance related to Sunny Hill?"

"He is her uncle."

"Thank you. Would it be possible for me to take this photo? I promise I will return it to you as soon as I make a copy."

"You may keep the photograph. I have many others."

"Thank you very much. This is going to be very helpful. Can you think of anything else, Mrs. Goldman?"

"Please, call me Song Lee." Then she laughed.

Besides the sigh in the living room it was the first sign of emotion Nattie had seen from her, but it came at an odd time.

"I am sorry to laugh with you, but telling you my name is Song Lee sounded funny to me this time."

Nattie just waited for her to explain.

"Song Lee is not a Vietnamese name. It is a Korean name. But Dicky and the Dogs could not say my Vietnamese name, so I became Song Lee. For the last thirty-five years I have been Song. Tomorrow I will fly to Denver. My sister lives there. There are many Vietnamese people in Denver. I think I will get my Vietnamese name back."

"Would you teach me your Vietnamese name? I would very much like to pay you that respect."

She looked at Nattie through slightly moistened eyes, "You are a respectful woman. I am honored that you ask me what I want." They tipped their heads at each other. "Today, I am honored to be Song Lee Goldman."

CHAPTER 12

The McDonald's on Midlothian

STEPPING UP TO THE COUNTER NATTIE ASKED, "I'm trying to meet with a group of men who I'm told eat breakfast here quite often. Do you know the group I mean?" When she talked to Abe Applewhite on the phone, he had given her directions to the McDonald's on Midlothian Avenue, but she had passed another one on the opposite side of the street on the way to this one. She was not confident that she was in the right place.

The dreadlocked cashier looked up and stared expressionlessly at Nattie. Then he glanced over her shoulder and tipped his head back in a motion that meant "Come closer" if the forehead was read or "Look over there" if the chin was read.

Nattie read the chin. She turned to find a distinguished-looking black man standing behind her. Short gray hair and a well-trimmed mustache, also gray, accented a warm face with clear brown eyes and just a trace of a smile. He was dressed in green pants, a white polo, and a dark green windbreaker. "Are you looking for a bunch of old men?"

"Not old, early sixties."

Her answer brought him to a chuckle. "Well, young lady, if seventy-year-old coots is what you're looking for, then I think we can satisfy you. The rest of the Pack will start straggling in here any minute now."

"The Mac Pack," chimed in the cashier.

The man behind Nattie chuckled again. "That's us all right, the Mac Pack. So, what does a pretty young lady like you want with the old Mac Pack?"

"I'm a private investigator from Bristol looking into the deaths of your friends Richard Goldman and Herman Ellis." Nattie handed him a business card and waited for the familiar response.

The crease in the middle of his forehead puckered as he scrunched his eyebrows together and studied her business card. "Dick," he finally said without looking up.

"Excuse me," she stalled. She had prepared herself to explain the Natasha McMorales reference, but it had not come.

"My friend's name is Dick Goldman." Sighing he placed the business card in his jacket pocket. "How can I help you, Miss Moreland?"

"I'm not really sure what would help, but I'd like to talk to you about what happened if that is OK. I'll buy breakfast."

"Are you on an expense account?"

"I am."

"So who is really buying my breakfast?"

"Bristol Motor Speedway."

"Well, thank you, BMS," he said, stepping around Nattie. Then to the cashier, "What's the twofer today, Mal?"

Malcolm had to turn around and look at the marquee menu to remember. "It's two for one on the sausage biscuits with eggs today, Ozzie."

Looking at Nattie, Ozzie raised three fingers. "There are three of us. Shall I order three or four?"

"Four, please," responded Nattie.

Ozzie winked at her and turned toward Malcolm. "Four of those and four coffees. She and I will have ours now, and then when Grey and Larry get here you can give them theirs. Is that OK, Mal?"

"You want it your way, is that it?"

"This is Burger King, isn't it?"

CHAPTER 13

Ozzie Applewhite

OZZIE LED THEM TO A TABLE AT THE BACK of the small dining area. The table had a bench seat on one side facing a television playing Fox News across from two chairs. "How's this?"

"Will the other two gentlemen find us here?"

"First of all, with the obvious exception of me, of course, we are not gentlemen. And second, do you really think that a beautiful twenty-year-old blond woman sitting here with a seventy-year-old black man will go unnoticed by anybody?"

Nattie circled the table, taking the seat next to the one Ozzie was standing behind. "Who am I to question the judgment of a seventy-year-old man?"

"Who indeed?" he snickered as he sat down next to her.

"I heard the cashier call you Ozzie, but that is a nickname, isn't it?"

"Why? Don't I look like an Ozzie?"

"The only Ozzie I know of is Ozzy Osbourne, and you don't look like him. No, I just don't have an Ozzie on my list. Are you Grey Troutman?"

Again he chuckled, "No, I'm not Grey, but he and I are the two 'colorful' members of the Pack. I'm Abe Applewhite." He took the lid off of his coffee cup and began unwrapping his breakfast sandwiches. "I suppose I look even less like an Abe than I do an Ozzie."

She took her moleskin notebook from her bag and placed it on the edge of the table. She unwrapped one of her biscuits as she watched him. His hands were big, but he had a delicate way of using his fingers as he adjusted the contents of his sandwich and applied an even layer of strawberry jelly on one side of the biscuit. She knew that technically it was a racist generalization, but it still seemed true that one difference between black people and white people was the ability to eat finger food without getting filthy.

With biscuit in hand he turned toward Nattie and asked, "Tell me, what is this list you have with our names?" Having put the conversation in her hands he began to eat.

"It's a list I got from the Bristol P.D. detective."

"I see," he said. "So Larry, Grey, and I are on your list, right?"

"Yes. Is there anyone else here in the Richmond area that you think I should talk to?"

"Well, if I was investigating a crime I believe I'd want to talk to Dick's widow."

"I went to see Mrs. Goldman yesterday morning."

"Really?" He sounded surprised. "You saw Song Lee yesterday? In the afternoon?"

"I did. It was the only time she could meet with me. She said she is going to Denver today, to be with her sister."

Ozzie shook his head slowly, "Wow."

"What?"

"Yesterday afternoon was Dick's funeral."

"Wow," Nattie agreed. "You would never have known she had just buried her husband."

"I knew she was one stoic cookie, but that's really something. She didn't shed a tear at the service. I just assumed she had cried herself out all morning." Ozzie's head remained still as he stared off at something in his thoughts.

Nattie waited until he began moving again. "How was the service?"

"It was small but nice. Dick wasn't a church person so it was at the funeral home. Song Lee had a few friends with her. I think they were from her church. It's a Vietnamese church. And there were two couples I didn't recognize. They may have been neighbors. And then there was us."

"How well would you say you knew Mr. Goldman?"

"We were in the service together forty-five years ago, and we've been working together and traveling together ever since. I suppose I knew him very well."

"What can you tell me that might help me find out who did this to him?"

Ozzie looked inquisitively at her.

"What?"

"Your question struck me as funny. The police asked us where we were and if we knew who did it. Your question is just . . . I don't know . . . different."

Nattie held eye contact with him as she waited for him to continue.

"We've talked about it." Raising his eyebrows, "Actually we haven't talked about anything else, and we've got no ideas. When Herm got it—" He looked at her. "I'm sorry. Do you know about how Herman died?"

"Mr. Ellis?"

He nodded. "He was murdered at Bristol Motor Speedway, too. Did you know that?"

Nattie nodded.

"It was at the August race in 2011. And then the next race at BMS is when Dick was killed. And you do know how they both died, right?" he asked again.

"I do."

"Brutal," he said, looking down.

"That seems to be the word everyone uses," noted Nattie.

"We were all shocked when Herm died. We thought it was just a crazy person he met in a bar or something. Forty years ago we were full of piss and vinegar, but the years had taken that from all of us except Herman. He was still a wild man."

"So you think he might have made the wrong person mad?"

"We thought that for a while, but nothing ever turned up. Eventually we just assumed it was an arbitrary act of lunacy. You know, big crowds attract all sorts of freaks."

"What about the means?"

"The means?"

"How he was murdered. Did how he was murdered figure into your lunatic theory?"

"We figured whoever it was, was either really crazy or really pissed off."

"Pissed off at Mr. Ellis?"

"Or pissed off at men."

"Was he the kind of person who could have made someone that mad?"

"I don't see how it matters now."

"Do you mean now that it has happened again? To someone else?"

"Yeah. I mean, even if Herman could have made someone that whacked out, Dick couldn't have. He was the nicest, most gentlest guy you'd ever want to meet."

"So you don't think it could be personal at Mr. Goldman."

"No, I don't."

"Could it be personal against your group? What do you call yourselves, the 'Mac Pack'?"

"We were the 'Dog Pack' back in 'Nam. We let Mal call us the 'Mac Pack' 'cause he likes it."

"Could it be a personal grudge against the Dog Pack?"

"It sure looks like it, doesn't it?" Scratching the back of his head, "But so far no one has a clue as to what it could be. It's got us all spooked about going back to Bristol. Do you think you can help us out?"

"I'm going to do my best to figure out who is doing this to you. I just need to answer several why questions."

"Why those two and why that way?" he offered.

"And why Bristol."

"Yeah, why Bristol?"

CHAPTER 14

Grey Troutman

"TELL ME ABOUT THE DOG PACK," SAID NATTIE, watching Ozzie finish off a biscuit.

"What do you want to know?"

"There were twelve of you, right?" asked Nattie. There were twelve men in the photograph she had gotten from Song Lee Goldman.

"Eight," he answered. "There were eight of us that started working fairs and carnivals together." Tipping his head to the left he added, "That was about forty years ago."

"OK, there were eight of you, and you all worked together, right?"

"Yes, but it goes further back than that. We were all in 'Nam together. We were a supply unit stationed just outside of Saigon. Basically we ran a warehouse for perishable items. Mostly we got large shipments of produce and meat, and distributed it in smaller shipments around the country. None of us had any plans when we came home, so when this vendor thing opened up it was just a natural fit for us. So we stayed together."

"How did it work? Did you have your own tent or something?"

"We've got several tents and three food wagons. There's a Bar-B-Q wagon, a weenie wagon, and an ice cream truck. We pretty much take those wherever we go. Then there are souvenir tents, and those change depending on where we're going and what we have to sell."

"That's quite an operation."

"It is."

"Is it profitable?"

"It has been."

"It *has* been profitable?" she repeated questioningly.

A higher-pitched voice from in front of the table asked, "Who you got here, bro?"

The question startled both Nattie and Ozzie. Neither of them had seen the man approach. He was slender except for the half a basketball peeking from under the white T-shirt that was a size or two too small. His short Afro was flat on the left side, looking like he had not touched it since waking. The lime-green golf pants looked like he slept in them as well.

As Nattie noticed his big toothy smile and lecherous stare, she realized he was considering what to say next. *Just spit it out, old man, so we can get past it,* she thought.

"Grey," Ozzie said, "this is Natasha Moreland. She's a private detective from Bristol."

Grey, who had been leaning forward across the table from Nattie, stood up straight and focused his attention on Ozzie. "From Bristol?"

Ozzie nodded yes. "She bought us breakfast. Mal has yours."

"Bought us breakfast. That's nice." Pulling his T-shirt down, "I guess I'll go get it."

As Grey went to the front counter Ozzie leaned toward Nattie. "I told you this has us all spooked. If you hadn't been connected to this investigation, he would have asked you if you like black men."

"Is that his line?"

Ozzie shrugged and lifted his eyebrows in the affirmative.

"Does it work for him?"

Ozzie's eyes twinkled, "Often enough for him to keep using it."

Grey must have gone to his car while he was getting his breakfast, because when he returned he was wearing a tan jacket zipped up to the neck. He sat in the seat directly across from Nattie. "Thank you for breakfast. So you are doing the investigating. Got any leads yet?"

"I was hoping you might have one for me."

Grey looked up from his struggle to get all the melted cheese from the wrapper of his biscuit.

You want to lick that cheese off that paper, don't you, Grey? wondered Nattie.

"She's just getting background so far, Grey," Ozzie said in an exaggeratedly calm voice.

You just rescued me, realized Nattie, as she watched Ozzie hold Grey's attention.

"That was a real nice service yesterday, Ozzie." Grey lifted his coffee cup in salute. "Maybe we should call you 'Deacon.'"

Ozzie turned to Nattie and explained, "I did the eulogy for Dick."

"He did it up good, too," added Grey.

"I'm sure he did."

Handing Grey Nattie's business card, "Natasha and I were just talking about the Dog Pack when you got here, Grey."

Nattie put her coffee down and took a deep breath. "Natasha McMorales is the name of the agency. I'm Nattie Moreland."

"I'm sorry," Ozzie said immediately. "I thought you were Natasha."

"So where's this Natasha chick?" asked Grey. "Why isn't she here?"

Both men waited for an answer.

"There is no Natasha McMorales. I'm the owner-operator. You are currently looking at the entire detective force."

After the two men glanced at each other, Grey pointed a fist at Ozzie and said, "So you are Natasha."

Ozzie tapped Grey's fist with his own. Then, gently patting Nattie's shoulder, "How about we call you 'Natasha' anyway? We like 'Natasha.'"

Thank you once again, Kevin. "OK." Then pointing at each of them she added, "But you two better not hold anything back from me."

"We've got nothing to hide, Natasha," offered Ozzie.

"Me either," added Grey. "In fact I'll strip down naked right here right now if you want me to."

Nattie turned her head slowly toward Ozzie, "Is that a new line?"

"He's never said that to me."

"Do you think it's going to work?" still addressing Ozzie.

He smiled, "Too early to tell."

"OK, Grey. Since it seems you have nothing to hide, why not tell me what you think?"

Grey grinned broadly and, pointing at himself, asked, "You want me to tell you who did that to Dick?"

"Of course I do. Do you know who did it?"

"I do," he boasted. "I've got it reckoned out."

"Are you serious?" asked Nattie.

"He's serious, but it's crazy."

"Crazy? Or genius? You tell me, Ozzie."

"No, Grey you tell me. What do you have against them?"

"Excuse me," interrupted Nattie. "Crazy or not, if you have an idea about this, I want to hear it."

Grey smirked at Ozzie and then, now that his audience had been established, settled back to tell his story at his leisure. "When a dude gets his thing cut off, you look for a woman, right? Like that Bobbitt woman, right?"

Nattie did not respond.

"Come on, Natasha, you're looking for a woman, aren't you? A woman who thought his thing belonged to her. A woman who wanted to punish him for what he did with it."

"Those thoughts have been considered, of course, but—"

"Who's crazy now, Oz?" interrupted Grey.

"Keep going, Grey."

He looked back at Nattie. Once he had eye contact with her again he leaned forward against the table. "Since everyone knows that looking for a woman is obvious, then it would be a perfect way for a couple of dudes to get away with it."

After a moment of silence Nattie realized that Grey was waiting for the question. "Do you have an idea about who these dudes are?"

"Here we go," crooned Ozzie.

"She asked," Grey strutted.

"So tell her."

"Yes, Grey, tell me. Who do you think is doing this?"

"It's those Dobbs boys."

Nattie scowled, trying to remember where she had heard that name. She began flipping the pages in her moleskin until she came to the list of names. "Are you talking about Lucas and Robert Dobbs?"

Sitting back and smiling, "Yep."

"Aren't they part of the Dog Pack?" Nattie asked.

CHAPTER 15

Larry Yarborough

A SHADOW FELL ACROSS THE TABLE, drawing the attention upward. He was standing right next to Nattie, so to see him she had to look virtually straight up. Even still it seemed his face was very far away. From that angle he looked to be ten feet tall with a huge frame and sunken, anorexic features, giving him an appearance like a morph between Frankenstein and a Ken doll.

"Larry Yarborough, meet Nattie Moreland," Ozzie said.

"We call her 'Natasha,'" added Grey.

"You bought breakfast." The voice was deep, sounding like it came from an empty oil drum.

"I did," said Nattie.

His extended hand looked like a baseball glove from when the Cubs last won the World Series. "Thank you."

Nattie's hand disappeared into his. His hands were calloused, but his grip was surprisingly gentle.

He circled the table and sat in the chair next to Grey. Nattie was sure that had they been at a newer McDonald's with the seats all affixed to the floor on posts, he would not have fit.

He unwrapped one of the biscuits and removed more than half of it with his first bite. With all that in his mouth he could still clearly ask, "Are you the detective from Bristol?"

Nattie nodded.

"How did you know that, Lurch?" asked Grey.

"He took Song Lee to the airport this morning," explained Ozzie before asking Larry, "How was she doing?"

Popping the rest of the biscuit into his mouth, "She's like she was yesterday. She's not going to fall apart in front of anyone. It's not in her."

"But it has to be bothering her," Grey said, looking to Ozzie for confirmation.

"Of course it's bothering her. How could it not bother her? When I walked her to her terminal she asked me if I thought Dick was faithful to her."

Grey sighed and looked at his empty hands. "I didn't think of that."

"What did you tell her, Larry?"

"I told her that Dick was the worst liar in the world."

Grey looked up with a jerk. "Did she buy that?"

Larry shrugged.

"But Dick was the best poker player in the Pack. He was a great liar."

"We know, Grey," agreed Ozzie, "but she wanted to know if he was faithful and he was. You did good, Larry."

Larry nodded expressionlessly. "She told me to tell you thanks for yesterday. She said Dick would have appreciated everything you said."

As she suspected, Ozzie did not look in her direction as she watched for his reaction out of the corner of her eye.

As she turned her gaze across the table, she caught Grey Troutman watching her watch Ozzie.

He grinned. "So, Natasha, you ready to talk about the Dobbs boys?"

Nattie flipped her notebook open again and scanned for the names. Lucas Dobbs was listed at the top, but Robert did not follow Lucas directly, which satisfied her concern about not remembering that there were two of them.

A hand, finger extended, blocked her vision. "What is that list?" It was Ozzie's finger.

"That's the Dog Pack," she answered, but seeing his face contort as he looked, she questioned, "Isn't it?"

The moleskin notebook was pulled out from under her hand. "Let me see that," demanded Grey.

"That's not the Dog Pack," Grey declared, pushing the book back toward Nattie. "More like Reservoir Dogs." He chortled and scanned his comrades looking for approval, an "amen," or acknowledgment of his wit. None came.

"Where'd you get that list, Nattie?" Ozzie asked.

"It's the list the Bristol detective gave me. I assumed she got it from one of you. She said she talked to all of you before you left town."

"She did."

"The blond?" queried Grey. "Yeah, she talked to us. I told her I'd confess to anything she wanted if she'd frisk me."

I'm sure she thought it was as funny as I do.

"How about I take off my shoe and shove it down your throat? Would that shut you up?" Larry's voice was as unemotional as it had been earlier, but his size and the resonance of his deep voice gave the statement a fairly menacing quality.

Grey looked at his friend, his forehead a mass of wrinkles, "Man, why do you have to disrespect me like that? I'm just trying to add a little levity to the festivities."

Larry turned his giant head toward Grey, "It's offensive. You wouldn't want me to talk to your mother like that."

Larry pointed at Nattie's untouched second biscuit. "Are you going to eat that?"

"It's yours," she slid it to him.

As Larry opened his third biscuit, Grey opened his hands up. "Would you tell Lurch here that women today aren't like the women he remembers from when he was in school?"

"Actually I think it was kind of nice. Thank you, Larry."

Larry nodded without looking at her.

" 'Thank you'! What are you thanking him for?" Grey's voice was excited as he jabbed his thumb toward Larry. Then to Larry he added, "By the way, big man, if you said that to my mother she would kick your ass."

Without glancing at Grey, Larry slowly slid down the bench seat and stood. Standing for a man that size was an ordeal. He reminded Nattie of one of those shadows that rise up out of a grave during a Halloween movie. Either that or he was severely arthritic. "Ozzie," he said, tipping his head toward his friend.

"Larry," returned Ozzie.

"Ma'am," another tip of his head to Nattie, "thank you for the biscuits." Then he ambled around the table without a glance at Grey.

For his part, Grey was silent as he watched the giant man circle the table and exit the restaurant.

"What's with him?" Grey asked innocently.

Ozzie looked at Nattie with wide eyes and his head tipped slightly to the right before responding. Nattie took the look to be an apology. *Maybe for airing their dirty laundry in front of me,* she reckoned.

"You know he's been sensitive about how women are treated since what happened to his daughter."

Pulling his head back and jutting his jaw forward, Grey spread his hands out. "Well, I didn't do it to her."

"He knows that," Ozzie chuckled. "I'm sure he'd let you know if he thought you did it."

"Is he a violent man?"

"Not even close," answered Ozzie.

"But if he was," Grey tapped the table, "he'd be good at it."

"Yes, he would."

"I can see that," Nattie paused, wondering if she should ask the question or not. "What happened to his daughter?"

Ozzie hesitated, "She was . . . She was. . . ."

"She got raped," said Grey, finishing what Ozzie could not.

The word was hard for Nattie, too. Like most women she wanted to believe that it could not happen to her, but when she was forced to think about it, she knew that if safety was a puzzle, it would always be missing pieces.

"That's awful. Did they catch who did it?"

Both men shook their heads in the negative.

"He's been real sensitive ever since it happened."

"Too sensitive, if you ask me."

Ozzie flinched his eyebrows as he eyed his friend. "I don't think he's going to ask you, Grey. Do you?"

Grey dismissed the question with a flip of his wrist. "I just wish he would stop jumping all over me."

"Well, come on now," said Ozzie as he settled back in his seat, "How many times are you going to take a bite out of the wrong end of that jelly doughnut?"

CHAPTER 16

The Dog Pack

WHEN THE LULL SETTLED IN FOLLOWING THE DISCUSSION about Larry's daughter, Nattie decided it was time to return to business, "So tell me about the Dogs."

"The 'Dog Pack,'" corrected Ozzie. "We got that name in 'Nam. Our unit was stationed just outside of Saigon. We ran a food distribution center. It was pretty simple work and a sweet gig when shipments were on time and there was enough food for everyone."

"How often would you say that was, Deacon? Twice a month?"

"If that." The two men bumped their fists together across the table before Ozzie turned back to Nattie. "The army prides itself on how it feeds the troops."

"The recruiters tell you, 'No matter what else is going on, you'll eat good.'"

"And it's true," added Ozzie in a more serious tone. "They work hard to see to it that everyone is well fed. I know. We did it. But there's no way that the volume of food we handled could come in and go out everyday with the timing that would make everyone happy."

"And if they weren't happy, we'd get blamed."

"We got blamed a lot."

"A lot," echoed Grey.

"Working together like that, under those conditions, brings you together. Especially when you are all taking undeserved heat."

"You guys handled all the food going into Vietnam. That's incredible. And there were only eight of you, right?"

"Oh, heavens, no. That would have been impossible. Our unit handled beef. There were units that handled fresh fruit and vegetables. They took more heat than we did."

"They deserved it," added Grey. "They ran their business like a black market."

"We don't know that for sure, Grey."

Pointing at Ozzie, Grey leaned toward Nattie. "The choirboy here likes to believe in the best of people."

Ozzie shrugged. "There was a unit that handled canned goods and another that handled dry goods. Those were the two biggest units. Our unit had twelve."

"I thought there were eight of you?"

"Eight of us stayed together after the war, but there were twelve of us over there."

"Did the 'Dog Pack' name come here or back in Vietnam?"

"'Nam."

"And the eight of you that stayed together kept the name, right?"

"We didn't get together right away. When the war ended we all went our separate ways."

"There's Justin 'Dok' Dokter," said Ozzie. He signed up for another tour when they told him they'd give him medic training. He's an EMT now down in Indian Trail, North Carolina."

"We called him Dok before he did all that EMT training," added Grey. "Do you think he goes by Doc Dok now?"

Ignoring Grey, Ozzie continued, "And Kent Paulette, he's from Hickory, North Carolina. He's an artist now."

"He's great," observed Grey. "What's the name of his website again?"

"Derfla," answered Ozzie. "And then there's Roscoe Phillips. He's an Italian professor down at U.T. in Knoxville."

"He changed his name again, Deacon."

"What is it now?"

"Sorceo."

"Is he a wizard now?"

"No, and he's not teaching Italian anymore either. I think he's teaching grade school."

"And lastly there's Michael Wade. He always wanted to be a fighter, so when he came back he figured he was in as good a condition as he could be. He had a short career before tearing up his rotator cuff. What's he doing now, Grey?"

"Retired, like we should be, Deacon. I think he ended up teaching high school up in Lexington.

"Dobbs was the one who had the connection to vending. His people had been hopping from county fair to county fair ever since he was little."

"He grew up on the road."

"So after the war he went back to what he knew."

"And he took Ike with him."

"Ike?"

"Ike Simmons."

"He had to take Ike with him," snorted Grey.

"Why was that?"

"Because the Sarge couldn't make it on his own."

"We always called him 'Sarge,'" explained Ozzie. "He was our sergeant in 'Nam."

"And he was still our sergeant once we were Stateside. Ike was his corporal."

"Ike was *our* corporal." To Nattie he added, "Dobbs was a warrior. If there was a conflict or even the hint of resistance to something we were doing he'd be front and center. Nothing was ever going to get in our way if he had anything to do about it."

Grey laughed. "Do you remember when we ran into that Green Beret bunch at Lilly's?"

Ozzie nodded. "Lilly's was a dive in Saigon we used to drink at. One day some boys we didn't know came in and were giving Larry a hard time." To Grey, "I don't know if they were Green Berets or not." Then back to Nattie, "That's the kind of detail that gets exaggerated."

"Shit. Deacon."

"Come on. Grey. You know it's true. None of us were there except Larry."

"And the Sarge."

"Yeah. And the Sarge. But he'd never let the truth stand in the way of telling a story. Especially if the story was about him."

With a smirk Grey kept his eyes on Nattie. "I noticed you never said anything like that to him, Deacon."

"Well, I never believed everything I heard, but I did believe everything I saw. And I saw plenty. By the way, brother Grey, I talked to Lilly about that fight."

"And?"

"And she told me it was three guys. She didn't say they were Berets, but there were three of them. Larry was sitting at one of those tables by the pool table." To Nattie, "The only lights in the place were over the cash register and over the pool table." Back to Grey, "Anyway, those boys wanted Larry to move, but he was sketching something on that notebook of his so he needed the light. According to Lilly they were on top of him trying to take his book when Dobbs walked in."

"Here we go," said Grey with an excitement in his voice that told Nattie the action would come quickly.

"Old Dobbs, he just took that club Lilly kept behind the bar. She called it her bill collector. He dropped one guy from behind and when the other two turned to face him, he took another one out with a homerun swing to the face. So before they knew what hit them, two were down for the count."

Grey laughed.

"So when you say he had a fight with three Green Berets, you don't picture what I just described, do you?"

Nattie shrugged and nodded.

"Do you know what your problem is, Deacon?"

"I know some of my problems." Winking at Nattie, "I'm too good-looking, and I hang out with the wrong people."

"Your problem is that you think too lofty for reality."

"Are you going to get philosophical on us now, Grey?"

"Seriously, you don't count that as a fight with three guys because he didn't follow the Ike DeQueensboro rules."

That was a Kevinism, thought Nattie.

"So tell me how I should think about it."

Tapping his finger on the table once, "He figured out what it would take to get it done and he had the salt to do it." Sitting back, "Most people don't have it in 'em to take out those first two boys like he did."

"Thank God for that."

"But he did."

"He did," agreed Ozzie. Turning again to Nattie, "And that brings us back to Ike Simmons."

"The corporal," noted Nattie.

Nodding the affirmative, "Old Dobbs was in charge. He decided what we'd do," said Ozzie. "Don't get me wrong now, he wasn't a tyrant with us. He'd ask our opinion."

"Sometimes," added Grey.

"And we could talk him out of things sometimes."

"Maybe you could, Deacon. And Ike could. But do you think I ever talked him out of anything?"

"Did you ever try?" asked Ozzie.

84

"Why would I?"

Raising his shoulder, Ozzie tilted his head to the left. "Like I said, he wasn't a tyrant, but he was authoritative."

Grey leaned once again across the table toward Nattie, "Wanna know what 'authoritative' is?" Without waiting for an answer he continued, "It's a slick tyrant."

With a long sigh, "Can I continue about the corporal?"

"Go ahead, Deacon. I'm not stopping you."

"As I was saying. Ike was the details person. He kept the books, made the orders, did all the paperwork. He made sure everything worked right, and if you had to talk to the Sarge about something, you always did it with Corporal Ike. And that was the way it was in the vending business, too. Ike held it all together."

"Hell, man," said Grey impatiently, "tell it like it was. He counted the money."

Nodding, "He counted the money. That says something about him, too. We all trusted him with the money."

"The money?"

"Yeah. Our money."

"We had a unique financial arrangement," explained Ozzie. "When we'd go to an event."

"Like the Bristol Motor Speedway?"

"Yeah, or a county fair."

"Or that giant garage sale in Hillsville."

"We might take two, three, or even four trailers. That would depend on what we got permits for. And whatever money we got we'd put into a single pot and Corporal Ike would divide it up."

"Everyone got equal shares?"

Grey snickered at Nattie's question.

"No. Ike got one and a half shares."

"He deserved it," said Grey.

"He did. We worked twenty-four events a year together. So we got quite a bit of time off. But Ike did a lot of his work while the rest of us were off. We all thought we got a deal with him."

"Besides, no one else wanted to do what he did." Grey thought a moment and asked, "Hey, Deacon, did Corporal Ike ever play poker with us?"

"Not on Pack-n-Play night." To Nattie, "That's what we called it after all the tourists left. We'd close up shop and do as much packing as we could while we had enough daylight. And then we'd play poker while Ike took care of business. One of us would do it with him, but for that we took turns."

"Yeah," agreed Grey. "One of us had to sit with him while he did all that stuff. But I never counted or anything. I just sat there with my headphones on and watched him."

" 'Pack-n-Play.' Isn't that a portable playpen?"

"I think so. Dok came up with the name. He helped us out once when we needed some extra hands. He had a bunch of kids."

"Now it makes sense," observed Nattie, "Pack means pack, and play means—"

"Poker!" repeated Ozzie in a sports announcer's voice.

"Ladies," added Grey in a voice mimicking Ozzie's.

With an embarrassed grimace, Ozzie explained, "There are always women around these kinds of events who . . . ah . . . want to. . . . "

"Play?" Nattie offered.

A trace of a smile grew across Ozzie's face as Grey laughed heartily.

"Yeah," Grey finally said, "they want to play."

"Sometimes the money counting would take a few hours longer than the packing. They'd go pay for the sites for the next race, settle up with anyone we owed money to, and they'd set money aside for maintenance and other expenses."

"Why would that take so long?" asked Nattie.

"Do you have an idea what fifty thousand dollars in quarters and one-dollar bills looks like?"

"It looks like several hours of work," noted Grey.

"What are you talking about, Grey? You never had to do it."

To Nattie, Grey grinned, "Nobody trusted me with the money."

"Nobody trusted anyone but you to take care of the vehicles," Ozzie told Grey.

"So who is the money person now that Ike Simmons isn't?" asked Nattie.

"Sunny Hill," answered Ozzie.

"Really, Sunny."

"Yeah, Sunny. Why does that surprise you, Natasha?"

I met her, thought Nattie. *I wouldn't think she could handle it.* "I'm not sure. I guess it's surprising that the job didn't go to one of the original Dog Pack guys."

"Are you kidding?" asked Grey. "Ike was the only one of us who could count past ten."

"Actually Ike picked her himself to take that over when he retired," said Ozzie. "And he was right. Her mind is like a steel trap."

"I don't know why I haven't thought of this before, but how did Sunny become one of the Pack? You said Ike picked her. Was she connected to him?"

Grey gave a concerned look to Ozzie, who kept his eyes on Nattie. The stiffness in his gaze told Nattie that her question had hit a nerve in each man.

"Sunny is Red's niece. He took her in when she was eleven. Her father was Red's brother. Her parents were killed in a fire."

"He was cooking meth," explained Grey.

Ozzie nodded his agreement. "She's got a couple of little brothers who were taken in by other relatives, but nobody wanted an eleven-year-old girl."

"How awful for her," said Nattie with a frown.

"I'm sure it bothered her, but she never showed it. She was one tough little girl," observed Ozzie.

"And she could work, too," added Grey. "I don't mean we violated any child labor laws or anything, but when she traveled with us she could work as hard as any of us."

"True," agreed Ozzie. "In those days she just went with us during the summer. She started with us full-time right after she graduated from high school. And like I said, Ike started right away to groom her to replace him when he retired."

"And he was right, too. She doesn't miss anything," said Grey. "Do you remember when she caught the money that Bobby was holding out?"

Ozzie nodded, "She's sharp alright."

Grey's eyes got big as he sat up straight, "Hey, man, I just remembered something." His eyes went back and forth between Nattie and Ozzie before he jabbed a finger in Ozzie's direction. "On the night that Dick Goldman was killed, do you remember who counted the money with her?"

Ozzie answered Grey while looking at Nattie, "The one who counted the money with Sunny that night was Dick."

"That's right," shouted Grey. "It was Dick. And on the night Herman was killed, he was the one who counted the money with her, too."

CHAPTER 17

Grey Troutman's Theory

"THAT'S QUITE A COINCIDENCE," observed Nattie.

"It is, Ozzie. I never trusted that girl," said Grey excitedly. "She's too quiet. And she watches everything like a hawk."

"Come on, man. It's not Sunny."

"What about that knife she always carries?" Turning to Nattie, "She keeps a stiletto in her back pocket. I've seen her pull that out and stick it under a guy's chin in a heartbeat. She's faster than lightning."

Leaning forward against the table, "Look, you two. Sunny may be a little different, but she's no killer." To Nattie, "If you were working with a bunch of dirty old men late at night, wouldn't you carry a knife?"

"But still, Ozzie, how do you explain this? Every member of the Dog Pack who counted the money with her in Bristol got his ....," she hesitated, searching for the right word. "Got hurt the same way," she finally said.

"I don't know how to explain that, but that doesn't mean she did it. Besides, if you remember, Grey, Dick played poker with us after they finished counting the money that night."

Grey exhaled loudly. "That's right," he admitted.

"So you both saw Dick Goldman between the time he was with Sunny and his death?"

Both men nodded yes.

"What about Herman Ellis?"

They looked at each other a moment before Ozzie said, "That was too long ago. I don't remember."

"Me either."

Changing gears, "Grey, you said something about the Dobbs boys. Tell me more about them."

"Yeah, them. To us they are Junior and Bobby, but that's who I meant. Why?"

"I want to check out every possible lead, so if you have a theory about them, then I'd like to hear it."

"Here we go," muttered Ozzie out of the side of his mouth.

Dismissing Ozzie with a wave of his hand, Grey began, "Don't mind him. He doesn't have a suspiciousioning mind like we do."

Ozzie rolled his eyes.

"You see, everyone is thinkin' it's got to be a woman, right?"

"Okay."

"So if you were a dude wanting it to look like a babe did it, you'd do something that would make everyone think, 'A dude would never do that.'"

"That makes perfect sense, but what about a motive?"

"Yes, Grey, what about a motive?"

Leaning back he smugly replied, "A snake don't need no motive to be a snake."

"I can't argue with that," conceded Ozzie with half a smile.

"Me either," agreed Nattie. "I'll check the Dobbs boys out. Do either of you have any other theories?"

"Not me," answered Ozzie, then glancing at Grey, he raised his eyebrows.

"Me either." Then looking at Nattie, he asked, "How about you, Natasha?"

Nattie unhooked her shoulder bag from over the back of her chair and placed it in her lap. After a brief search she withdrew the photograph she had received from Song Lee Goldman. Placing it flat on the table she said, "I'm glad you asked. What can you tell me about the redheaded man?"

Both men leaned over the photo, looking at it much longer than was necessary to recognize who the redhead was. Grey was the first to raise his head. "Oh man, it stinks to get old. I gotta go get rid of that coffee." Without looking in Nattie's direction he stood and headed toward the back of the dining room where the men's room was located.

Ozzie also avoided looking at Nattie when he lifted his head. Instead he watched Grey disappear into the men's room.

"I guess it's just you and me, Ozzie."

Turning slowly to face her, "What would you like to know?" His voice was low and weaker than it had been only a few minutes earlier.

"My understanding is that he was one of the original members of the Dog Pack. Is that right?"

"Yes."

"I suppose there's an explanation for why you omitted his name when you gave me the Dog Pack roster."

"There is. I guess it's just easier for us to forget about him. He was one of us from the beginning. We went through boot together." He looked down and to his left. "It was a shock to me when he got arrested." Lifting his head he added, "It was a shock to all of us."

He looked directly at Nattie for the first time since she placed the photo on the table. His focus moved back and forth from one of her eyes to the other before he spoke again. "I never would have thought he'd do something like that."

"Something like what, Ozzie?"

He inhaled deeply, "Don't you already know?"

"I'm sure I can find out what the public record is, but I'd like to hear what you have to say about it."

Staring directly at her, "I wasn't there. All I can tell you is that he was arrested for drugging and beating up a hooker, and then leaving her for dead. They gave him sixty years, which was the max."

"Did he do it?"

Shrugging, "He confessed."

CHAPTER 13

Weaverville, North Carolina

"YOU DID PROMISE WE'D GET TOGETHER when you got back from Richmond, Nat," said Nathan with a touch of whine.

In the not-so-distant past the tone alone in Nathan's telephone voice would have triggered a wave of guilt in Nattie. But this was a new day, and now what was triggered was merely an awareness that it had once had a power over her. "I did not promise that the minute I got back I'd call you, Nathan. I got back late last night, and I have to go to North Carolina today."

"What's so urgent in North Carolina?"

"I have to interview an elderly woman there. Her daughter told me it had to be today, or I'd have to wait several weeks."

"Why is that?"

"I didn't ask."

"Okay," he said in higher pitch. "Where are you going in North Carolina?"

"Weaverville."

"Weaverville, great. It's just over the mountain. I'll go with you."

"Nathan!"

"No, really. My whole day is open. I'll ride along with you. We can have lunch in that diner we like. What was the name of that place again?"

"Do you mean the Stoney Knob Cafe?"

"Yeah, that's it. That's Weaverville, right?"

"I think so."

"That's the place with the great sandwiches, the Greek diner, air conditioning, and the eclectic artwork."

When they were married, Nathan and Nattie had spent a weekend at the Hot Springs Health Spa near Weaverville and had gone to the Stoney Knob Cafe for dinner on Saturday. On the advice of the staff at the Hot Springs they had gone early to miss the rush that dinnertime would bring. While they waited for their food, which was as good as had been promised, they enjoyed what Nathan had called "the widest range of wall art styles in the Western Hemisphere." What Nattie remembered was a small replica of the Venus de Milo statue, longhorn steer horns, a painting of the Last Supper, a Buddha figurine, and a stuffed sailfish. It was a good memory.

"What will you do while I'm at my appointment?" she asked.

"I could go with you," he suggested. "I was a detective, too, once. Remember?"

"Ahh . . . ," she hesitated.

"I'm kidding, Nat," he said quickly, rescuing them from the awkward moment. "I'll just go to a coffee shop or something. It'll be okay."

Two hours later they sat on either side of a booth near the front door of the Stoney Knob Café. Nathan had ordered the Southern Comfort Panini, which came with fried green tomatoes, smoked bacon, and havarti cheese. Nattie's affection for all things Italian came through in her choice of the Panini Michelangelo, which came with grilled chicken, buffalo mozzarella, and pesto.

Nattie was thankful that during the drive over the mountain their conversation had been superficial. He talked about his bar, the Our

House Tavern, and his sobriety, a subject of great interest to her as she blamed his alcoholism for the dissolution of their marriage. He asked her about her work, the case she was working on, and her family. When she retold the story of Kevin's theological insight followed by his Old Testament reference of going to "Beer," Nathan had laughed heartily. His laugh was one of the things she most missed, and while he was lost in the laughter she could watch him without being noticed. She had always thought he was too good-looking for her.

These are dangerous feelings, girlfriend, she had reminded herself as they drove.

She was not sure what she wanted, or maybe she did know what she wanted but was unsure of whether she could have it. Either way, the one thing that she was sure of was that she did not want to be trapped in a car having the "define the relationship" talk. Their marriage had been disastrous. Their divorce had been amenable. An attempt to nurse him back to health after his nose was broken trying to protect her went too far, too fast. And their only public date ended with harsh words and him driving off angry. So, if anything else was going to happen between them, she was determined to make sure it happened very, very slowly. She was sure of her resolve, but her confidence was weak.

While they waited for their food to arrive, Nathan leaned forward with a serious look across his face.

Nattie could feel the muscles on the back of her neck tighten. She knew what was coming.

"What would your family say if we started dating again?"

"My family? Don't you think that what I think is more important?"

Frowning, "Come on, Nattie, you know what I meant."

"Tell me what you meant."

"I meant that I know how important your family is to you. I was concerned about the grief you might take if we started dating again."

"Is that what we're doing, Nathan?"

"I'm hoping that's what we're doing. It's what I want anyway. What do you want?"

"I want to be healthy, and I want my life to matter."

"Okay, I'm up for that. Do you see me fitting in to that goal?"

"Do you?"

"Honestly, Nat, I can't see anything else."

"Look, Nathan, I'll always love you. No matter what, I'll always cherish our marriage. But I'm not sure what kind of future we can have."

He started to speak, but she waved him off before she could begin. "I do know this, Nathan: I can't be your whole life. I tried to make you my whole life before, and look where that got us."

"What happened to us was not your fault, Nattie."

"No, it wasn't. But I didn't help either."

"It can be different."

The sound of a woman clearing her throat broke their concentration. "Who gets the Southern Comfort?" she asked.

Nattie pointed at Nathan, and the waitress placed the oversized platter in front of him. Nattie's meal was next; it was as large as Nathan's.

"I'm going to go ahead and tell you I'll need a take-home box."

"Do you want me to bring it now?"

"Sure."

"And how does yours look?" she asked Nathan.

"I think I'll be able to finish mine."

She smiled. "Don't forget to save room for dessert."

When the waitress was out of earshot, Nattie leaned forward. "Let's just start with occasional dates and see where that leads, okay?"

"No problem. I'm all about taking it slow."

"Good."

"So, Nattie," he said lifting his panini to his mouth, "what are you doing tomorrow night?"

CHAPTER 19

Angie Simmons Taylor

AFTER DEPOSITING NATHAN AT THE WELL BRED BAKERY in downtown Weaverville, Nattie retraced her route from the Stoney Knob Café until just past Lake Louise, where she turned on to West Lakeshore Drive. Nattie had made the appointment with Michelle Simmons's daughter, Angie. It was Angie who had given her the directions and the advice to stop at Well Bred. "They have the biggest chocolate-covered cream puffs you'll ever see," she guaranteed.

She followed Angie's directions, and five minutes later she parked in front of a small brick home with a lavish flower garden. As she walked to the front door she could hear a dog bark. It was a single bark, deep and strained, and it came from a large brown mutt lounging in the shade of the front porch. The dog watched Nattie approach without lifting his head. He did not even lift his head when Nattie bent over to pet him.

"Are you a watchdog?" Nattie asked as she strummed her fingers behind his ear—a gesture that earned her one slow wag of his tail.

"That's Bluto," explained a woman's voice from inside the front-door screen. "He's the doorbell."

Standing up, "I'm Natalie Moreland from Bristol, Tennessee. Are you Miss Simmons?"

"I'm Angie Taylor, Simmons is my maiden name," she said, stepping on to the porch. "I'm Michelle's daughter."

"Are you who I talked to on the phone yesterday?"

"That's right. I'm just here from Chattanooga for a few days to help Momma get moved to an assisted-living facility. That's why we had to meet today or wait a good while because I was hoping to head back home this evening. I've got some little ones of my own to get back to."

"I understand. I'll try to be quick."

Angie smiled and opened the door. "Come on through the house. We're enjoying the backyard one last time." Once they were both inside, Angie turned to Nattie, "I just want to explain about Momma. She's got chronic osteoarthritis and the beginnings of dementia."

"I'm sorry to hear that."

"Well, thank you. But you need to know that her memory isn't so good, so I don't know how much she'll be able to help you."

"Thanks for letting me come and try. I'm sure this is a busy time for you."

Sweeping her arm around the living room, "As you can see we haven't done any packing. We were going to, but it became clear in a hurry that it will go much faster once Momma isn't here. We're just relaxing. We went to the beauty parlor this morning and down to Asheville for lunch. And we have a four o'clock appointment at her new place later today." Then, scanning the living room again, she said, "It looks like I won't make Kershaw until tomorrow night."

Nattie looked at her watch. It was 2 p.m. "I'm sure I will be gone well before your four o'clock meeting."

Angie nodded and started moving through the house again. "The timing is good. She's having a good day, and this will take her mind off the move. Besides, her favorite thing to talk about is Daddy."

The back patio was well shaded by a green-striped rollout canopy. Around the edge of the patio were several small flower boxes with little red petunias and yellow marigolds. The backyard was very small, but it teemed with shrubs and flowerbeds. At the corner of the patio stood a five-foot metal frame with what looked like a pot on the bottom with a half dozen of wires strung between the pot and the top piece. The gentle breeze not only cooled them off but it seemed to make the strings ring in a kind of New Age musical chant.

Michelle Simmons sat in a wicker glider and watched Nattie notice the music. Her hair was teased out, and her makeup morphed her fair skin into rosy cheeks. Her lipstick, a subdued shade of red, covered her very thin lips. Her smile revealed an almost too-white row of front teeth.

"Do you know what that is?" Michelle asked.

Nattie moved closer to the structure. "No, I don't. I don't think I've ever seen anything like it."

"My Ike gave it to me on our fiftieth wedding anniversary. It's an aeolian harp."

"It's lovely. Your whole back yard is lovely."

"This is the detective from Bristol, Momma," Angie said. "She called yesterday and asked to talk to you about Daddy's group."

"So you're from Bristol?"

"Yes, ma'am."

"King College, right?"

"Yes, it is."

"Did you go to King College?"

"No, ma'am, I didn't, but it is a fine school."

"That's where my Angie went."

Nattie looked at Angie, who was still standing in the French doors leading to the patio. "Class of 2000."

"She was on the basketball team," said Michelle proudly.

Angie shrugged, "That's me. I rode the bench as well as anyone ever has." Then squinting she asked, "Do you know if Michelle Williams is still the coach?"

"I'm sorry, I don't know," apologized Nattie. "I think they're pretty good, though. They're in the Bristol paper a lot."

"That's okay," Angie said. "I was just wondering. Don't let me keep you from doing what you need to do with momma."

"So you want to know about the Dog Pack," said Michelle. Pointing at a glider sitting empty next to her, she said to Nattie, "Come sit here, my dear."

As Nattie sat down Angie announced, "I'll go make us all some lemonade."

"Thank you for meeting with me, Mrs. Simmons."

"Oh, please, call me Mike. Everyone calls me Mike."

Angie, who was in the kitchen, heard that through the open window. "I don't call her Mike."

Mike kept smiling at Nattie as if she had not heard Angie at all. "Tell me your name, dear."

"Natalie Moreland is my name, but most everyone calls me Nattie."

"It is nice to meet you, Nattie. And it is nice that someone so young as you would be interested in some old Vietnam War vets. So tell me, what would you like to know about the Dog Pack?"

"Have you kept in touch with any of your husband's partners recently?"

"No, I haven't. We were pretty close to the other families when Ike was still traveling with them. We lived in Kingsport then, and so did the Dobbses. Everyone else lived in Richmond. But when Ike retired we moved here to North Carolina. I guess we just lost touch after that. The last thing I heard about any of them was when Louis Dobbs died." Raising her voice, "Wasn't that about two years ago?"

"I think it was just last spring, Momma," answered Angie from the kitchen.

"That was a little more than a year ago," translated Mike. "Is everyone else still doing well?"

A movement in the kitchen window behind Mike caught Nattie's eye. Angie was waving her hands and shaking her head "No." Guessing that Angie had chosen not to tell her mother about the deaths of Herman Ellis and Dick Goldman, Nattie decided to avoid the question. "I can't say much about that. I'm really here to find out about something that happened over twenty years ago."

"I don't understand," declared Mike. "Why did you ask me if I was still in touch with any of them?"

You got me, thought Nattie. *You're much sharper than your daughter led me to believe.* "I don't know, Mike, I suppose I was just making conversation."

"Well, it seemed like there was something going on recently that brought you here."

"I can assure you that my questions are all about the past."

Mike continued to stare at Nattie. She was still smiling, but the suspicious look remained as well.

Nattie retrieved the photo of the Dog Pack from her shoulder bag and handed it to Mike, who took it and immediately smiled, "I have this picture, too." Leaning toward Nattie slightly, she pointed, "That's my Ike."

"Yes," said Nattie, assuming Mike was pointing at Ike. Mike's gesture to hold it out for Nattie to see was considerably insufficient.

"Where did you get this?" asked Mike. Then turning it over she observed, "This is Song Lee Goldman's handwriting."

"Like I said, Mike, I'm investigating something that happened over twenty years ago. I did get this from Mrs. Goldman. I had asked her about Reed Hill. Do you remember Mr. Hill?"

"Red?" she repeated, holding the photo down in her lap. "Of course I remember him."

"According to her, Mr. Hill went to prison for hurting a woman. Do you remember that?"

"I do. It was horrible, what happened to that woman. I would never have thought Red would do such an awful thing."

"That's exactly what I want to hear about."

"I'm not sure that I can tell you more than Song Lee has already told you." Michelle folded her hands in her lap and smiled sweetly. She was ready to talk about something else.

"I asked Mrs. Goldman to tell me what the awful thing that happened to that woman was, but she could not."

"The woman was a prostitute," said Mike nonchalantly. "I assume what happened to her is what happens to prostitutes. But apparently after that happened, Red took her home and left her for dead."

"Mrs. Goldman seemed to think that there was more to it than whatever Red did."

"Well, I wouldn't know anything about that. It happened when my Ike was counting the money. Nonetheless, he was heartsick over what happened. Things were never the same after that. He used to love those men, but after that he couldn't wait to retire and move away." Handing the picture back to Nattie, "I honestly believe if Red hadn't gone and done that, we would have retired closer to Kingsport. That's where Lou Dobbs retired, but Ike wanted to be away from all of them."

"Thank you for that. It was quite a bit more than Mrs. Goldman could tell me. She also told me that your husband had a habit of keeping a very detailed daily diary."

"That's true," chimed in Angie, who had returned with a tray of lemonade, each glass sporting a sprig of mint. "Daddy was famous for his record keeping."

"I don't know about that," replied Mike, as Angie handed her a glass.

Nattie noted the look of bewilderment on Angie's face as she received her glass. "Thank you. This looks fresh squeezed."

"It is," answered Angie. "The mint is from Momma's garden, too."

There was an awkwardness that hung in the air as the three women sipped their lemonades and discussed the various flowers planted around the yard.

"This has been very nice," Nattie finally said, "and I know I've kept you long enough, so if I could just impose on you for one more thing, I'll be on my way."

"What's that?" asked Angie for her mother.

"I'd really like to read your husband's diary from that time period."

"That's no prob—" started Angie before Mike interrupted her.

"I'm afraid that is no longer possible."

"Why, Momma?"

To Angie, Mike said, "I didn't keep those diaries." Then turning to Nattie, she added, "I'm sorry. I wish I could have been more help."

Angie looked at her mother like she was seeing her for the first time.

CHAPTER 20

The Burger Bar

THE BURGER BAR, ON THE CORNER OF STATE STREET and Piedmont, is a Bristol landmark. It's a tiny place with a counter for ten and tables for eleven inside. As one would expect, the Burger Bar specializes in burgers. Their real claim to fame is that on New Year's Eve in 1952, country singer/icon Hank Williams is said to have had his last meal here. He died in the backseat of a Cadillac hired to drive him to Ohio. The back wall of the Bar is adorned with photos from that time period along with a framed memorial *Bristol Herald Courier* article written by Joe Tennis.

"I'm surprised you wanted to eat here," noted Nattie as she and Marissa arrived at the door simultaneously.

"Really, why is that?"

Wondering if her question came off as judgmental, Nattie hesitated. She had never been here for breakfast before. Her visits to the Burger Bar had been at lunchtime, and only when she was in the mood for a burger. Her usual was a B Z Burger, which came with a fried egg, onion, and secret spice, which Nattie took to be cayenne pepper. Kevin preferred the Fire God Burger. She liked Kevin's burger's heat but not its volume. It was huge, and for food you ate with your hands, huge meant needing to take a nap after you ate, and it often meant taking your clothes to the cleaners too.

"I don't know. I just never thought of this place for anything besides burgers. But it does look like you could get a pretty good truck-stop breakfast here."

"It does," agreed Marissa, holding the door open. "And sometimes a good truck-stop breakfast is all that will do."

"Hi," greeted Shelly from behind the counter. "How are you all?" Shelly was twenty-something, with long, dark hair, glasses, and a baby-blue T-shirt with the Burger Bar logo on the back and the Rhythm and Roots logo on the front. "We're out of biscuits this morning, but you can substitute pancakes if you want."

They sat next to each other below the Hank Williams memorial while Shelly brought coffee and water to the table. Marissa ordered the two-egg breakfast combo with pancakes. Nattie ordered Chef Armond's Breakfast Burrito, telling Shelly, "I hope the salsa has some legs."

"Before you tell me about your trip to Richmond, let me tell you about the ME's report," Marissa said quietly.

"Dick Goldman?"

Marissa nodded.

"Roofies?" asked Nattie referring to Rohypnol by its street name.

"Yes. I know we assumed so, but now it's confirmed. Now, tell me, how was your Richmond trip?"

"I met with Mrs. Goldman the day of the funeral, and then I met with Applewhite, Troutman, and Yarborough the next morning."

"What did you find out?"

Taking out her moleskin pad, "For one thing the list of people you gave me is the current Dog Pack. Are you aware that they are not all part of the original Dog Pack?"

"No."

"I didn't think so. The name 'Dog Pack' actually goes back to Vietnam, where they all served together." Handing a sheet of paper she had withdrawn from her shoulder bag to Marissa, "Here's a copy of a photo of the original group."

Marissa studied the page. In the center was a color copy of the photo Nattie had gotten from Song Lee Goldman. Around the edge Nattie had written their names. Pointing at Louis Dobbs, "Is he the father of Lucas and Robert?"

"Yes. He was the sergeant."

"In Vietnam?" asked Marissa.

"And here, too, I think. They still called him 'Sarge,'" then pointing at Ike Simmons, "and they called him 'the Corporal.'"

Marissa continued to study the photo. "How old is this picture?"

"Forty years."

"This guy doesn't look much different."

Nattie leaned forward to see that she was touching Grey Troutman's image. "He's got a theory about who the murderer is."

Marissa looked up at Nattie and waited.

"He thinks it is the Dobbses."

"Okay," said Marissa. "Does he say why?"

"The way they work is to pool all the money and then divvy up shares."

"So, the less people getting a cut, the bigger the shares for everyone else."

"I don't think Mr. Applewhite gave that theory much credence," said Nattie with a shake of her head.

"Does he have another theory?"

"No, not that he shared with me anyway."

Furrowing her brow, Marissa asked, "Do you think he's hiding something?"

"Sort of," Nattie answered. Tapping the picture, "Song Lee Goldman told me about this guy."

"Reed Hill," read Marissa.

"According to her, Red Hill—that's what they called Mr. Hill, 'Red'—Red was sent to prison twenty-some years ago for what she called 'hurting a woman.' She couldn't tell me much about what happened, but she did say that Ike Simmons, the Corporal, would have a detailed record of it in his diary."

"We'll want to track that story down then," stated Marissa. Noticing Nattie's grimace she asked, "What's wrong?"

"When I asked about what happened the Dog Pack guys got nervous. And I did go to Weaverville to interview Ike Simmons's widow, Michelle."

"Did you get the diary?"

"No, I didn't. And when I brought it up she denied that she kept his diaries."

"Was she lying?"

"I'd bet the farm on it, but why?"

"I don't know, but it'd be worth it to get the court records about that case."

"I agree," said Nattie. "And I'm guessing you can do that a lot easier than I can."

"Yeah, I'll get on that right away. Anything else?"

"I was thinking I might check out the Dobbs brothers myself, if you don't mind."

"Fine by me."

Shelly showed up with their food and coffee refills.

Nattie took one bite of her breakfast burrito. Her eyes widened and her lips formed a tight little zero.

With a slight chuckle Marissa observed, "I'm guessing you got your wish about legs."

CHAPTER 21

Lucas Dobbs

THE MUSTY SMELL STARTLED NATTIE as she walked through the open door. The exterior of the small corrugated metal warehouse looked like it had recently been power washed, so the condition of the interior caught her off guard. The lighting threw her off, too. The three old, dim lightbulbs dangling from the ceiling, the dust that seemed to hang in the air, and the fact that she had just come from the bright sunshine of midday combined to make her wonder if she had wandered back in time four decades. Along the left side of the open room were several small trailers. Two rows of shelving created an aisle along the right side of the building. After her eyes got used to the darkness she scanned the left side. Seeing no sign of anyone she moved to the end of the aisle, way on the right.

"Anyone here?" she called out.

"I don't want any," came a raspy voice from somewhere to the back of the building.

Making her way toward the back, she moved slowly to avoid the clutter that was spread out along the way in front of the shelves on either side of it. She looked down at a half-empty box of plastic tiaras as she stepped over it and onto a flat Budweiser sign lying on the floor next to it. The sign slid from under her. and after struggling to hold her balance for a moment she let herself fall backward. Fortunately she landed in a box of small stuffed frogs instead of the box of Dale Earnhardt shot glasses sitting next to it.

Not touching anything had been very important to her in the moment before she fell, but that was completely gone now that she was stuck in a V shape inside the box. Her legs, sticking virtually straight up and slightly spread, were no help at all as they flailed about in a vain effort to gain balance. Wiggling her upper body, she felt around with her hands looking for something, anything, from which to push herself up.

"I thought I told you I didn't want any." This time there was a body connected to the voice. He was standing in the doorway of an office at the end of the aisle. All she could make out about him from his silhouette in the doorway was that he had short hair, he was of medium height with a V-shaped torso, and he was wiping his hands on a rag.

Oh great, she thought as she watched him begin moving toward her. She stopped struggling to get up as she kept her eyes on his approach.

The angry, disgusted look on his face disappeared as he came to stand over the top of her. Looking down at her brought an expression somewhere between a sneer and a smile. It was the kind of delighted smile a spider might have looking at a fly caught in its web.

"Well, well, what have we here?" he said.

Holding out her hand, "Are you going to help me up?" *Or are you just a pig?*

"Help you up?" he repeated. Scratching his head, "I don't know. Why would I want to do that?"

Putting her hand down, she kept her eyes on him. She was at his mercy to some extent. Her gun, holstered at the small of her back, was of no use as it was still inside the box and her hands were not.

His smile shifted into a grin as he leaned forward, offering her both his hands.

She had no choice but to take hold of his hands. As soon as he got his grip adjusted, he popped her up and out of the box like she was a rag doll. He kept a hold on her hands as she flew through the air, unable to do anything other than allow her body to flatten against his. Their faces were three inches apart. He held her there against himself long enough to let her know with his eyes he was enjoying himself and that he had done it deliberately before letting her hands go.

As she finally touched the floor she shoved him away. "That wasn't okay."

"What?" he asked with a snicker as he turned away and headed back toward the office at the back. "I told you I didn't want any." Laughing harder, "I guess I changed my mind."

The picture of running up behind him and kicking him between his legs and then watching him roll around on the floor screaming in pain ran through her mind. The brief fantasy diverted her anger momentarily but did not lessen it at all. Still angry she asked, "Are you Lucas Dobbs? Or are you Bobby?"

Reaching the doorway he turned to face her. "I'm Lucas. So what?"

"So I'm a PI from Bristol, and I want to ask you a few questions about the murders of Herman Ellis and Dick Goldman."

Cocking his head to the left he looked at her and scrunched his face. "You're a PI?"

"I am. So what?"

Her bravado brought another smile to his face. "I've just never seen a lady PI before. Except on TV." Then pointing at her, "You know, you look like that Veronica Mars chick. What was her name?"

Kristen Bell, thought Nattie, but she was not feeling friendly enough with him to satisfy his trivia quest.

"Farrah Fawcett," he announced and puffed out his chest in pride.

Not even the same decade, you moron.

Waving a hand over his shoulder he retreated into his office. "If you want to ask me some questions, come on in."

She did not want to be alone with him in the warehouse, much less a more isolated inner office, but she was not going to let him know she was afraid of him either. Stopping at the doorway she surveyed the room. Sellable knickknacks spilled out of a bank of shelves along the right side of the room while a large cluttered desk sat catty-cornered in the back corner to her right. In front of the desk was a single straight chair, and behind that an old maroon couch with newspapers strewn over it. Lucas took the seat behind the desk, effectively cutting himself off from the rest of the room. Seeing his position, Nattie decided that she could sit across from him and still have a clear escape route if the need should arise. *Besides,* she told herself, *it wouldn't be so bad if I had to shoot him.*

"So, what do you want to know, Farrah?"

The thought of giving him her real name never crossed her mind.

"I want to know who killed Dick Goldman."

"And you want to know if I did it?"

"No. I know that the police have already talked to you and have verified your alibi."

"Well, that's good to know."

"I want to know anything you can tell me that might help me figure out who did do it. So, what can you tell me?"

"I can tell you what I think."

You think? Who would have thought?

"I think it was a woman. A man-hater with a grudge against those boys."

"Those boys?"

"Herman Ellis and Dicky Goldman."

"Are you aware of someone with a grudge against those men?"

111

He frowned, "Nah, but Bobby and I have only been around for the last few years. It could be some woman who goes way back with them. You know they were all in Vietnam together."

She nodded yes.

"So, that's all I know. Anything else?"

Before she could answer, the sound of something falling came from the warehouse.

"It's that damn cat," he blurted as he jumped up and sprinted from the room.

In less than a minute she heard something breaking. It sounded to her like something glass had been thrown against a wall. Then she heard him yell, "Go on, get out of here."

Then, as if coming out of a fog, she realized that he was now on the other side of her, trapping her inside the office.

Her two quick steps to the doorway were just a moment too late, as Lucas had returned. The spider grin had returned as well.

"You're not in a hurry are you, Farrah?"

Backing up she said, "It's time for me to go."

"Oh, you don't really want to go, do you?" Stepping directly toward her just enough, he closed the door behind him with his foot. "I was thinking we could get to know each other better. Wouldn't you like that?"

That's it, she determined with a sneer. Reaching around back with her right hand, she found that during her fall in the warehouse her holster had slid to the left, which required a more pronounced reach. She took hold of the object in her holster and, despite its strange feel, she withdrew it and pointed it at Lucas Dobbs.

"What the hell is that?" he asked looking at the small stuffed frog.

CHAPTER 22

Sunny Hill

WITH NO PARTICULAR SKILL LUCAS HAD RUN nearly over her, and while her focus was on staying upright he bear hugged her. Once her arms were pinned to her sides it was relatively simple for him to lift her up and take her to the edge of the couch. All he needed to do was keep his hips turned to avoid her kicks to his groin. Had she anticipated what he had in mind, her fear would certainly have gone up, but the only thing she was aware of as he walked her across the room was the embarrassment of allowing herself to be caught in such a vulnerable position.

The embarrassment did turn to fear when she felt herself falling backward onto the couch. His full weight landed on top of her. An "ugh" exploded from her as they landed. Had it not been such a cushy couch, she may have had trouble breathing. As it was, her fight-or-flight response kicked in, and she began again to fight to free her arms.

For his part, the fall initiated another strategy for Lucas. Pinning her arms required both of his, but now that he was on top of her he let his right arm go. He had other plans for his right hand.

Nattie used her free left arm to push his chin up and away from her.

He could have easily shifted to either side to get around her push, but it would have required letting go with his left arm. He chose to hold on, which kept their bodies locked together and his head forced painfully backward.

They stayed in that position for what seemed to Nattie several minutes. Her shoulder had begun to burn, and she knew her elbow would begin trembling any moment.

Finally a guttural chortle came from somewhere down his throat. "How long do you think you can keep this up, girlie?"

"As long as it takes, you pig. How long do you think you can go without breathing?"

"I'm breathing, sweetheart," he said, straining the words.

"Not very well. I'm just lying here listening to how hard it is for you to breathe with your neck in that position."

Although it was difficult to speak he managed to mumble, "Of course I'm breathing hard with you lying underneath me like this. I just wish you had a little more cushion on you, if you know what I mean."

The taunt triggered another surge of anger and adrenaline in her. She pushed even harder against his chin.

An attempt to laugh failed as his breathing was cut off even more. Then he realized his right arm had been doing nothing more than holding his weight away from the wall above the couch. Pulling his right hand from the wall he slowly fell to his right, but not so fast that he could not grasp her by the wrist and pull her hand from beneath his chin. The fall placed his full weight once again on top of her with his face nestled alongside her neck. He moaned softly into her ear.

Nattie's response to the moan was to pull her head away—a move he interpreted as revulsion, which made him laugh. But the laugh was short-lived as her real intention became clear. Her movement away from him was simply to create as much room and momentum as she could for a head-butt with the side of her head. The maneuver would have hurt her more than him if he had only stayed still. It would have meant she was hitting his hairline with her left temple. But he did not stay still. When she moved away, he rose up to watch her, making her poorly aimed head-butt a collision between the top of her head and the bridge of his nose—a much more effective maneuver.

"You bitch," he screamed. He got hold of each of her upper arms and squeezed as he held her down. The fingers biting into her arms sent shooting pains down through her elbows. He held himself directly over her face with his full weight on her arms. Leaning down close enough for her to feel the hotness of his breath he snarled, "I'm gonna hurt you." Then his red eyes got big.

"Not today, you ain't."

Nattie felt his grip loosen before she noticed the shiny steel knife that was cutting into his throat.

"Git offin her, Junior."

"What do you think you're doing, Sunny?" he asked without moving off of Nattie.

"It seems to me that I'm about to slice me a slab of bacon. What do you think I'm doing?"

"I think you're making a big mistake."

"I've made 'em before."

Nattie stayed very still and watched them stare at each other.

He made the first move. "You aren't going to do anything," he mocked.

Before he had finished speaking she withdrew the knife blade from his neck, flipped her hand over, and struck him in the temple with the handle. Before his first scream concluded she climbed on his back, wrapped her left arm around his neck, and inserted the point of the slender knife into his right ear.

"Get yourself up, Junior."

He raised himself up on his hands and knees but remained straddled over Nattie.

115

Pushing the blade farther into Lucas's ear brought a howl of pain.

"Get up *now*, Junior."

With a low growl he slowly lifted himself up, handling the extra weight of Sunny on his back as if it were nothing.

Gripping his hips with her knees, Sunny hung on like it was a pony ride.

Standing dead still in the middle of the room he raised his hands slightly. "You'd better kill me, Sunny."

"Is that what you're a-thinkin', Junior?"

"You don't think I'm going to forget this, do you?"

"I don't know, Junior. Do you think if I stuck this here knife way down in your ear that it might put a mess of varmints in your memory?"

The expression apparently made no more sense to Lucas than it did to Nattie.

"What the hell are you talking about?"

"There's no call for cursing now," she said with a calmness that belied her actions. Tightening her grip around his neck she scrambled up his back so that her face was beside his ear. While she did this she moved the knife from inside his ear to the front of his face. With cat-like speed the knife was repositioned so that it was now pointing straight at his left eye. The tip was so close to his eye that he froze.

"I'm thinkin' you might be right, Junior. Maybe I should go ahead and kill you."

"I don't think you want to do that, Sunny," offered Nattie.

"Really? Why would that be?"

"He may deserve it, but if you do it, it will bring trouble your way."

"It appears to me that trouble has already come my way."

"You're not a killer, Sunny."

"That may mean something where you're from, but where I'm from, killing vermin is no big deal."

116

"Put the knife down, Sunny." It was Marissa's voice. None of them had heard her come in. Nattie, who had been facing the door, had not noticed her entry either.

Without withdrawing the knife, Sunny leaned back to look at Marissa.

"I mean it, Sunny. Put down the knife and get off of him." Marissa's handgun was leveled at Sunny's face.

Nattie found herself watching yet another standoff, another battle of wills played for deadly stakes.

Marissa slowly circled the standing duo until she was in front of Lucas, facing Sunny over his shoulder. Keeping the gun leveled at Sunny with her right hand she reached for the knife with her left. "I mean it, Sunny. Let me have the knife."

"Why should I?"

"Because I'm going to shoot you in the face if you don't."

The comment brought another staring standoff.

"Besides," added Marissa, "I'm here to arrest this bozo anyway."

Grinning, "Now if you'd said that from the beginning we'd-a been a lot further along by now." She dropped the knife into Marissa's hand and hopped off Lucas's back.

As Marissa placed him in handcuffs behind his back, she recited his Miranda rights to him.

After nodding that he understood Lucas pleaded, "What are you arresting me for? I didn't do anything."

"Right now you're being arrested for trafficking in illegal substances."

"What are you talking about?" he sneered.

Raising a finger she circled around his desk as she put on a plastic glove she had stored in her jacket pocket. Standing in front of the middle drawer she asked him, "Do you mind if I open this drawer?"

"I do. So unless you have a search warrant, just back off."

"Well," she smiled, "it's a good thing I do." With that she withdrew the document from the inside pocket of her jacket and held it out to see.

His head and shoulders drooped as he exhaled loudly.

Opening the top left-hand drawer Marissa withdrew a metal box and sat it on the desk. "What do you suppose I'll find in here, Mr. Dobbs?"

Coming back to life a bit he growled, "You have no grounds for that search. My lawyer is going to have a field day with you."

"I wonder if that's true," she mused. "Your brother was arrested this morning for selling to an undercover police officer. I don't know how good your lawyer is, but he's going to have a hard time having a field day throwing out information your brother gave us. What do you think, Nattie?"

Stepping up to the side of the desk Nattie peered at the box. "What does he have in there?"

Marissa opened the box with her gloved hand. The box was full of label-less pharmaceutical bottles. Marissa lifted one of the bottles and held it up to the light. It was full of some kind of pill. Holding the base with her gloved hand she took a tissue from her pocket and opened the lid. "Roofies," she said as she peered inside.

After a quick glance at each other Marissa and Nattie turned their attention back to Lucas Dobbs.

Nodding toward Sunny he asked defiantly, "What about her? She was going to kill me."

"He was raping her," countered Sunny, pointing at Nattie.

"Is that true?" asked Marissa.

"It hadn't gotten that far yet, but it was headed that direction, and she saved me." To Sunny, Nattie added, "Thank you."

Sunny looked back at her without expression or response.

To Marissa, "He was going to hurt me. She stopped him."

"Well, Lucas," Marissa said, turning him toward the door, "there you go. That's not attempted murder. It's not even aggravated assault.

It was a Good Samaritan coming to the aid of a woman being victimized. Is that how you saw it, Nattie?"

All eyes turned to Nattie.

Staring directly at Lucas, Nattie said, "Yes. Isn't that how you saw it, Sunny?"

Sunny stared at Nattie for a moment, then turning to Lucas she said, "It is."

Lucas glared at Sunny but held his tongue.

"Smart boy," offered Marissa. "Exercising your right to silence is a good move. I wasn't sure you had it in you."

The glare shifted to Marissa.

"Let's go," she told him as she placed her right hand up under his left arm and pushed toward the door.

With a grimace he let her lead him toward the door. As he neared the door he leaned back for a last look at Nattie. Instead of a glare he blew a kiss at her—an action that would have outraged her had he not at that very moment also stepped on something that twisted his ankle, requiring Marissa to keep him from falling.

When he finally stabilized he looked down, and with a groan he kicked the little green stuffed frog into the warehouse.

CHAPTER 23

Debbie and Marissa at the Grind House

"YOU'RE A PRIVATE INVESTIGATOR," NOTED DEBBIE. "Can't you do anything about that?"

Nattie followed her gaze through the window of the Grind House to the freight train parked in front of the "Bristol, A Good Place to Live" sign.

"I mean it," continued Debbie. "How can Bristol function if the main street through town shuts down several times a day because a train comes to a dead stop? Can't they just go farther and stop?"

Nattie grinned and asked, "What do you think I should do about it?"

"I don't know, but someone should do something about it. What I don't understand is the stopping. It makes sense that traffic stops while it pulls through, but why does the whole town have to stop?"

"Are you okay?"

"Yeah," she replied innocently. "Why do you ask?"

Pointing at the stopped train, "Well, for one thing, that has been going on for as long as I've been here. Most of us just get used to it."

Lowering her voice Debbie grew more serious. "You know there's a gravel lot over past the train station."

"The one with the 'Private Property' sign?"

"Yes. Well, I parked over there once and waited for the train to stop."

"Nice detective work, Sherlock. What did you find out?"

Raising her eyebrows and lowering her voice even more, "There's a little house over there. That's where the engine will stop, and someone will get out and go into that little house."

"Oh my goodness, Debbie, do you think there's something sinister going on there?"

Frowning, "Well, what do you think is happening in there that can't happen farther down the tracks?"

"I assume it's some sort of office. The engine of the train may need to deliver papers or get new orders. For that matter, it could be a place to go to the bathroom."

Rolling her eyes, "Great, the whole town of Bristol shuts down for a half hour because last night the engineer had a bad batch of clams."

The Natasha McMorales Detective Agency office was located diagonally across State Street from The Grind House, making it a convenient place to meet for coffee. Nattie, as usual, sat near a window facing State Street so she could keep one eye on her office. Normally she would have seen Marissa Ferguson go into her office, but she had not noticed. She did notice Marissa exiting the office and making her way across the parking lot toward the Grind House. "Oh good," she said. "Here comes the police detective I've been working with. I'm glad you'll get a chance to meet her."

Debbie, who had been sitting with her back to the front door, turned in time to see the tall woman come through the door. "She does look just like Dharma," she observed.

Nattie waved her over.

"Who needs a refill?" asked Marissa at the edge of the table.

"I'm good," said Nattie.

"Me too," added Debbie.

"Marissa, this is my friend Debbie."

Debbie identified herself with a wave of her hand.

Marissa flashed a big toothy smile and extended her hand. "Hi, Debbie, good to meet you. Am I intruding?"

"Not at all, please join us."

"I can't stay but a minute," looking to Nattie, "but I've got something for you."

Nattie took the envelope from Marissa's hand. "What's this?"

"It's a letter of commendation. I put it in the case file, and I wanted you to have a copy."

Nattie stared at the envelope without lifting her eyes. She was embarrassed, and she knew that Marissa knew she was embarrassed.

"There it is again," said Marissa. "It's just too easy." She patted Nattie on the shoulder before heading to the counter.

Marissa took the chair next to Nattie when she returned to the table. The seat gave her a clear view of Debbie's unflinching concentration on the train.

Turning toward them, Debbie tapped her watch. "It's been twenty minutes. Can you believe that? Twenty minutes."

"Debbie is concerned that the train's shutdown of State Street is hurting the town," explained Nattie.

"I see."

"I think she's having a bad-hair day."

"Trouble at home?" asked Marissa.

"Oh, don't get me started," began Debbie as she turned to give her full attention to the two women sitting across from her. "I caught my husband throwing his T-shirt on top of the hamper this morning."

With a quick glance at Marissa, Nattie asked, "Isn't that a good thing? My ex never got a T-shirt anywhere near a hamper."

"The hamper was shut. The lid was down. He just threw his dirty stuff on top of it. Who do you think is going to pick it up and get it into the hamper?"

"Did you ask him that?" asked Marissa.

"I did. Do you want to hear his answer?"

"As long as we've gone this far."

"He said that since he keeps the lid on the john shut for me, I should keep the lid of the hamper open for him."

Nattie and Marissa looked at each other for a moment in a silent sort of eyebrow dance. Marissa began the dance with raising hers, signifying confusion, while Nattie's response was a lowering of hers, indicating she was just as much in the dark.

After catching their looks, Debbie rolled her eyes. "You're both single, right?"

"Yes, we're both single," acknowledged Marissa, "but besides that, it seems like he's got a point."

"I know I'd make that deal," agreed Nattie.

Debbie exhaled loudly as her shoulders slumped. "You're right. I know, I should be glad about what a good man he is. He works real hard to make a life for us here, and it isn't easy getting his practice started."

"What does he do?" asked Marissa.

"He's a dentist. A really good dentist. He's thorough, you know, he takes his time. He's gets some grief from the other dentist he works with because he's not faster, but that's the kind of man he is. And he's real good to me and our kids." With that, Debbie stood up. "Excuse me," she said as she headed for the bathroom.

As soon as it was clear that Debbie would not be back quickly, Nattie leaned closer to Marissa and said, "I know it's been awhile, but the last time you were in here you got a text and said you thought you were in trouble with your lieutenant."

After Marissa nodded her agreement Nattie asked, "So, were you?"

"Yeah," she said grinning, "he yelled at me. I had just responded to a domestic violence call without backup. He's right, that's not usually a good idea, but I knew who the guy was. It's a homeless man named Doug. I've dealt with him and his wife before. He's not the kind of guy who gets his kicks by beating up women. I tried to get him hooked up with social services, you know. I think he'd be alright if someone would help him with some skills."

"But still, Marissa, abuse is abuse, isn't it?"

"You sound like my lieutenant, only his line was 'Procedure is procedure.'" Holding up her hand as if to block the next line of argument, "I know, it's not my job to decide who the good guys are and who the bad guys are. If Doug is doing something bad, then I should treat him just like he was anyone else."

"If you ask me, Marissa, I'd say your lieutenant is trying to look out for you."

"Yeah, I know." Then pointing toward the bathroom she asked, "What was that all about with your friend?"

"I think she was trying to convince us that her husband is one of the good guys."

Looking toward the back of the coffee shop Marissa wondered, "Are you sure it's us she's trying to convince?"

CHAPTER 24

Return to BMS

NATTIE HAD NOT BEEN BACK TO THE SPEEDWAY since she had first gotten the job, although she reliably submitted her expense and progress reports every Monday morning. Until the last two weeks, payouts had only lagged behind her reports by a few days, but now that the Dobbs brothers were in custody and a final check was due there had been no communication. Hoping the delay was simply an oversight, Nattie decided to drop by the BMS office and inquire about the delay.

"Hi, Pam," Nattie said, stepping up to the counter. "Do you remember me?"

"Of course," Pam beamed with a big smile as her eyes searched for a recognition.

"I'm the detective they hired. . . ."

"The murders," Pam said, pointing at Nattie excitedly. "It was those two boys, right?"

Tilting her head, Nattie saluted the BMS grapevine's effectiveness. The arrest was only three days ago, and the identity of the Dobbs brothers had not yet been released, but Pam knew nonetheless.

"I really can't comment on that, but I'm sure it will be in the papers soon enough."

"Well," she shrugged, "I heard it was two brothers. Oh, well. At least it's over before this coming August race. What can I help you with?"

"I'm not real sure who I need to talk to, Pam, but I'm missing a couple of checks, and I don't know who to talk to about it."

Scrunching her eyebrows together, "Would it be Payroll?" she asked herself out loud. "I'll try Accounting."

Nattie listened as Pam explained her situation to someone.

"Okay," Pam finally said. Hanging up the phone she looked up at Nattie. "They said to wait. Someone will be down in a minute."

Pam's phone rang again, so Nattie stood in the plantless atrium and watched a tour group load into a white van for a lap around the track.

It was closer to seven minutes before someone tapped Nattie on the shoulder. "Miss Moreland?"

Since she had expected someone from Accounting, she was surprised to see a familiar face.

"Cami," she introduced herself with a warm smile and an extended hand. "Emma sent me to get you."

"Emma," repeated Nattie. "Why Emma?"

"She didn't say. She's waiting for you in the conference room." Cami led Nattie toward the elevator.

"How are things going this year?" asked Nattie, wondering, *Did bad press about the murders hurt attendance this year, and is Emma going to blame me for it?*

"Tickets sales for the August race have been the best we've had for the last few years," answered Cami. "The state of the economy is effecting us, there's no getting around that, but we're riding it out. There was some talk on the Internet about stock cars and heat racing, but I don't know if we'll go in that direction."

"Will that be Mr. McElroy's decision?"

Cami smiled, "You know, Jeff Byrd, our former general manager, used to tell us, 'Bruton Smith's name may be on your paycheck, but don't ever forget for one minute that the body of race fans is our boss.'"

Emma Iverson stood behind the conference table with her arms folded. On the table in front of her was a closed executive notebook. The pen to the left of the notebook was placed perfectly parallel and centered. "Please have a seat," she said, pointing to the chair directly across from her.

"Good to see you again, Emma," Nattie said, holding out her hand.

Emma put her hand into Nattie's grip but did not return the squeeze. "I'd prefer to be called 'Ms. Iverson,' if you don't mind. Business decorum is getting to be such a lost art, don't you think?"

"If it's lost, then I say 'Good riddance,'" announced Cami, taking the seat at the end of the table. "Do you still call it lost if no one is looking for it?"

"Ms. Timmons Armbrust," said Emma sternly.

"Yes, Miss Iverson," answered Cami in a manner that sounded to Nattie like how the orphans said, 'Yes, Miss Hannigan,' in the movie *Annie.*

Nattie's involuntary smile disappeared as she noticed the lack of amusement on Emma's face.

"I think you have other matters to attend to, do you not, Ms. Timmons Armbrust?"

"Not at the moment," she said. "I was hoping to hear something that might go nicely into a press release." Sitting back she spread her hands out over her head like she was outlining a banner, "Bristol Motor Speedway teams with local detective Natasha McMorales to solve nationwide crime epidemic."

"I think not," glared Emma.

"That's what Descartes said."

Nattie could not hold back the laugh, which brought the same glare Cami had received.

"Please excuse us, Miss Armbrust," said Emma without taking her eyes from Nattie.

"Is there a problem?" Nattie asked innocently as Cami shut the door behind herself.

"Not necessarily. There are a few items on your expense report that I need to go over before we make the final payout. You don't mind answering a few questions, do you?"

"Not at all. What would you like to know?"

Opening the notebook Emma scanned what Nattie could tell was the first expense report she had submitted. "I see you spent several days in Richmond."

"That's correct."

"Most of your receipts are from the Midlothian area."

"That's true."

"I understand from your report that you interviewed the widow of the last victim and three surviving vendors who all live in that area."

"Those interviews eventually led us to the arrest."

"I'm sure your contribution was appreciated by the official law enforcement designee. However, I am inquiring about this last expense to Kuba Kuba."

"What about it, Ms. Iverson?"

"I lived in Richmond while my husband was in medical school at MCV, Miss Moreland. I know where Kuba Kuba is. It's in the Fan. That is a far cry from the Midlothian area. Do you expect the Speedway to underwrite your social life?"

Feeling the tension tighten the muscles in the back of her neck, Nattie fought off her defensiveness. "That lunch only cost about $25."

Lifting the page, "It cost $32.75."

"I took Mr. Applewhite and his wife out to lunch at a place of their choosing."

"And how did that expense further your investigation?"

"The truth is that it did not generate anything useful, but I could not know that without doing it. Surely you understand that not every lead I follow will be fruitful."

"And surely you understand that not every expense will go unquestioned," snapped Emma. "I know how you work."

"Excuse me," Nattie said, firmly holding her right index finger up. "What do you mean, you know how I work?"

"I did not mean you, per se, I meant private investigators in general."

"Well, what do you mean by that in general then?"

"I mean you generally make your living spying on people."

"There's a certain amount of that, that PIs do, but how does that have anything to do with this case or my expense reports?"

Raising her eyebrows and looking down, "I can only imagine that working for us would look like a cash cow to someone who normally hides in the shadows trying to take dirty pictures."

"And you thought I might be trying to take this cash cow for $32.75?"

Emma narrowed her eyes and inhaled. The retort never came, though, as Mac McElroy, the director of the Speedway, entered the room.

"Miss McMorales," he exclaimed. "Well done. Well done indeed." He stood leaning on the right end of the conference table, his silk tie dangling. "I can't tell you how pleased we are that this matter was resolved before the August race." Turning toward Emma, "Aren't we, Emma?"

"Relieved," Emma said warmly without looking at Nattie.

"Yes, relieved," agreed Mac. "Relieved that we don't have to worry about explaining another one of these . . . these . . ."

"Murders," offered Nattie.

He closed his eyes. "That's such an awful word." Shuddering, he added, "I'm glad it's over. Well done, Miss McMorales, well done."

"You already said that," observed Emma.

"But it bears repeating." Turning to Nattie, "Are they getting you taken care of?"

"We were," said Nattie slowly. Facing Emma, "We were just going over a few expense items."

"Oh, nonsense," Mac said quickly. "Emma showed me those bills two weeks ago." To Emma, "Have you told her about the bonus yet?"

"I hadn't gotten to that yet," sighed Emma.

Without noticing Emma deflate, Mac continued, "Oh, good, then I get to tell you myself. We decided to give you a thousand-dollar bonus if you got it done before the next race." Standing back up he proclaimed, "And you did. Congratulations."

"Thank you, sir. It is an unexpected generosity."

"Not at all. Even with the bonus it is still much cheaper than the Jackie Ke Agency that we almost went with. They approached us the week after we hired you."

"The Jackie Ke Agency," repeated Nattie. "Out of Oklahoma?"

"Yes, I think that's what they said. Is Oklahoma right, Emma?"

"I believe so, sir," answered Emma.

Mac continued, "We would not have considered making a change except they guaranteed getting it solved before the August race. Solved, or they wouldn't have charged us a dime."

"That must have been hard to resist," observed Nattie. "Jackie Ke is a legend, and I'm sure she would have come through for you." Glancing toward Emma, who was looking down, "I wonder how she would have known about this case? She usually stays in the heartland. And it's odd she would have offered a guarantee like that. It's like she knew exactly what would tempt you."

"Well, tempted or not, we made the right choice. Right, Emma?"

"Clearly," agreed the sullen Emma Iverson.

"That detective over at Bristol PD—what's her name?"

"Marissa," answered Nattie. "Marissa Ferguson."

"Yes, Detective Ferguson told us that you were invaluable. Wasn't that the word, Emma?"

"I don't recall, sir." Emma looked sick to her stomach.

"Well, you have been invaluable to us. And you can be sure that if we ever have need of your services again, we'll be calling." Circling the table he shook Nattie's hand with both of his own.

Standing, Emma said, "If you will wait here, Miss Moreland, I will get your check for you right now."

"Well done, Emma," Mac said as Emma excused herself. Lifting his shoulders sheepishly, "I guess my word for the day is 'well done.'"

"Well done," agreed Nattie.

CHAPTER 25

Nathan at Shooter's Edge

NOT NOW, SHE SIGHED TO HERSELF AS SHE ENTERED the lobby of Shooter's Edge, the indoor shooting range in Piney Flats. Nathan was sitting on the comfy couch to the left of the entry. He was reading the paper and, at least to Nattie's thinking, acting as if he wasn't waiting for her to show up.

"Enjoying yourself?" Nattie asked from where she had stopped. She was determined that she would not walk over to him. It had been over a week since he had tagged along with her to Weaverville. The day had gone smoothly enough, but he was as eager for more time together as she was hesitant. He had told her so on the drive back over the mountain. She had stalled him, saying that as soon as the case she was working on got resolved, she would be open to getting together again.

"I am," he answered. Standing up immediately he folded and tucked the paper under his arm. "At least I'm enjoying myself now that you are here." Strolling over to her he added, "I saw Kevin this morning over at Blackbird Bakery. He told me the BMS case was solved. I bet that feels good."

Shaking her head yes, "It's always nice to get paid."

"And now you're here to get some shooting in," he observed.

Holding the gun case in front of her, she asked, "What gives you that idea?" Sarcasm was her way to tell him she was unhappy with him. It had never been effective when they were married, but it was an old habit.

"Do you remember the first time we came here?" he asked.

Of course she remembered. It was a month after he had joined the Hiram Moreland Detective Agency where they had met. She was the receptionist, but with Hiram's encouragement she had begun the process of getting her own private investigator's license. Hiram hired Nathan, his sister's son, shortly after Nathan had received an MBA. Hiram had hoped that if Nathan could learn the business, he could better court more lucrative insurance jobs. It was Hiram's idea that they both get licensed to carry concealed firearms, and to that end he sent them to the Shooter's Edge with the charge to rent several guns and "see how they feel."

"That's right," she answered, as if the thought had just occurred to her. "This is where we came."

Laughing, he recalled, "Do you remember your first shot with the Ruger .38?"

On that first visit here Hiram had told them to just try the revolvers. "Save the automatics for another day," he advised. The attendant behind the counter gave them a .22 Smith & Weston revolver and two .38s, explaining that the .22 was the gun to start with, as it was quieter and had very little kick. Even with the warning, Nattie's first shot with the .38 had startled her such that she literally jumped up and launched into a nervous giggle.

"The Ruger LCR is the gun I mostly carry now," she told him.

"Really," he said, a touch of surprise in his voice.

"That, or the Glock .38."

His head pulled back slightly. She had never wanted any part of automatics when they were together, and now she had the Cadillac of automatic handguns.

"Can I join you on the range? I'd sure like to see how that Glock feels."

Hesitating she looked over her shoulder at the sales counter.

"You know what?" he said. "I can see that this is not a social time for you. How about a rain check?"

His sudden reversal caught her off guard. She was not accustomed to his noticing her subtle attempts to establish boundaries, much less his responding to them. "A rain check sounds good, Nathan. I hope I'm not being rude, but I like to run a box of .38 cartridges through each of my guns and be on my way."

"No problem, Nat, I understand. How about lunch? I found a Mexican place up in Abingdon you'd like."

"Lunch would be great Nathan. Wednesday?" As soon as she heard herself agree to the lunch date she wondered how it had happened again.

"Wednesday it is. I've been looking forward to a real date since we went to Weaverville. I'll see you then." Tipping his head he headed out. As he reached the door he stopped and, turning back, asked, "So, Nattie, tell me. When did you get that Glock?"

"A while ago I took it from a guy who wouldn't stop pestering me."

CHAPTER 26

Pentecost Sunday

"I'M GLAD YOU SUGGESTED SAHIB'S, KEVIN," said Ingrid. It was their monthly go-to-church-and-have-lunch Sunday. "We almost never come here anymore." Sahib's is a restaurant in Johnson City specializing in Indian cuisine. The buffet, which is only served at lunchtime, was a common eating place for the O'Brien clan when they all lived in Johnson City. It had become a forgotten favorite once Nattie and Kevin moved to Bristol. If they all gathered for lunch anymore, it was either a holiday or it was the monthly after-church lunch. The after-church lunches were always held at the O'Brien home, and it was not because Ingrid was eager to cook. It was because of Lionel's habit of holding court over that morning's sermon.

"Why is that?" asked Lionel as he sat his salad down at his place.

Nattie and Kevin looked immediately at Ingrid. If anyone was going to tell him the truth it was hers to do.

"We usually have Samantha with us, and she doesn't care for this," replied Ingrid. Samantha, Lionel's daughter from his first marriage, was out of town with her family.

I wonder if that's true, thought Nattie.

The conversation was scattered as they each had their own method for attacking a buffet. Lionel was the only one to begin with a salad. Ingrid got one small portion of something and leisurely ate half of it before doing the same thing with another dish. Kevin's approach was to load as much as he could on a plate, top it off with naan, and then do the same thing again. Nattie always started with "reasonable" servings of a lentil bean dish called daal, a potato and spinach dish called aloo, and something new, something she had never tried before. Suspicious of the color, she always stayed away from the tandoori chicken.

The unspoken family rule about the meal here was "every man for himself" during everything but dessert. If you were ready for dessert first, you waited for everyone else. Today Nattie and Lionel were the first ones finished. Technically Ingrid was finished also, but she was picking at the remains of something on her plate while Kevin made sure that no profit was made on him.

"Chai anyone?" asked Lionel. Turning without waiting for an answer he went toward a huge urn sitting on a separate table at the front end of the buffet.

Taking advantage of Lionel's absence Ingrid leaned toward Nattie. "So, how was your date yesterday? A new Mexican place in Abingdon, right?"

"Ouch!" cried out Kevin. Ingrid's question got him a knuckle punch to his thigh. "What was that for?" He had not heard his mother's question or seen his sister draw back for the punch.

The question earned him a glare from Nattie.

"He didn't tell me," confessed Ingrid.

"That hurt," whined Kevin rubbing his leg.

"Man up!" chorused the mother-daughter duo.

Nattie turned her glare on her mother. The glare was a maneuver that Nattie used sparingly. Overuse would diminish its effectiveness. It nearly always worked on Kevin and Nathan.

Ingrid smiled. She was impervious to the glare. It was a maneuver she had mastered long before Nattie had came along. "Nathan told me."

"Nathan? Since when are you talking to Nathan?"

"Since I discovered my daughter was still in love with him."

Please, Nattie prayed, *someone shoot me.*

"Really, honey, if you two are going to begin seeing each other again, why not bring him to lunch with us? Are you ashamed of your family?"

It was Nattie's turn to smile.

"Did I say something funny?"

"It's not that, Mother. It's just that the 'Are you ashamed of your family?' line used to make my stomach knot up. You're not losing your touch, are you?"

Ingrid responded in her best Blanche DuBois voice, "Why, I'm sure I don't have any idea what you are talking about."

"I'm not ready to include my family in my relationship with Nathan yet. I'm sure you will be among the first to know when I decide differently." *One way or the other, I'm sure,* added Nattie to herself.

Lionel returned with four cups of Chai. "So," he said as he sat, "what did you think of the sermon this morning?"

To Nattie, the question had always sounded a bit like he was requesting a critique of the sermon, but he was not. Once, when he was in high school, Kevin had responded by saying that it was too long and too dull. Lionel made it clear that a critique was not what the question called for.

It was Pentecost Sunday, so the sermon text was taken from the first few chapters of Acts. The focus of the sermon had been on the change in Peter from how he was portrayed in the Gospels and how he was at Pentecost. That was undoubtedly what Lionel wanted to discuss.

"I've got a question," announced Kevin.

"Great," replied Lionel.

137

This ought to be good, thought Nattie.

"When they had to figure out who was going to replace Judas, they had two guys they were considering, right?"

"Yes, Joseph and Matthias."

"And they picked Matthias, right?"

"Yes."

"Well, what happened to Joseph?" Holding up his thumb and forefinger an inch apart, "This guy came this close to being one of the apostles, and now, whoever heard of him?"

"That's not really the point, Kevin," scolded Ingrid.

"It might not be the point to you, but what about him?" Imitating Marlon Brando's voice from *On the Waterfront,* he said, "I coulda been an apostle."

"I'm ready for dessert," announced Ingrid, drawing the attention away from her son.

"Wait, I'm not done," continued Kevin, getting it back. "What about how he got skipped?"

"What about how who got skipped?" asked Lionel.

"Joseph. He came that close to being in the most famous group of all time, and he didn't get in because of what? Casting lots? What is that, some kind of dice game?"

"Kevin, you're being irreverent," scolded Ingrid.

"I'm irrelevant a lot, but this casting-lots thing seems like an endorsement for gambling."

"Cheese balls?" asked Lionel sternly as he stood up and returned to the buffet.

Nattie watched as Lionel walked back to the buffet. Then, turning to her mother she asked softly, "Was he cursing?"

Glaring at Kevin, Ingrid answered, "I wouldn't blame him if he was."

Kevin returned the look with the corresponding deer-in-the-head-lights expression, "I wasn't trying to be irrelevant."

"Let's all get dessert now," intervened Nattie, noting the effectiveness of her mother's glare.

Once they were all back at the table, each with their own small bowl of what looked like a donut hole swimming in honey water, Nattie shifted the conversation. "I was curious about something from church this morning."

The proclamation brought a double take from Kevin. When they were adolescents, Nattie would often take Kevin to task later for prolonging the Sunday after-church lunch discussions with questions and comments.

"I was in New Orleans last year on Pentecost Sunday. The reason I remember is that it was the middle of the afternoon and it was incredibly hot, so I went into a church that faces Jackson Square. I just remember it was air conditioned and the music was incredible, so I sat down and listened."

"That's nice," noted Ingrid. "What kind of church was it?"

"I guess it was a Catholic church. You would have loved it, Mother. There was a gigantic oil painting of Saint Francis hanging at the front."

"Over the altar?" Lionel asked tersely. His animosity toward Catholicism had been the reason Ingrid had abandoned her interest in the fourth-century Catholic saint.

Nattie's disappointment in her mother for letting him take that away from her was also the reason she began her own fascination with Saint Francis. "It's not over the altar. It's hanging over a doorway in the right corner of the front wall."

"I thought you were curious about something from our service this morning, Nattie," redirected Ingrid.

"I am. I heard an announcement about new members meeting in the parlor after the service, and I remembered last Pentecost, so I was wondering: is that a normal church practice?"

"What?" asked Lionel in a better tone.

"You know, a new-members' service on Pentecost Sunday."

Ingrid and Lionel looked at each other before Lionel answered. "I don't think I've ever really noticed that before, but it makes perfect sense, doesn't it?"

Ingrid nodded her agreement.

"After all," Lionel continued, "there were three thousand converts that day."

"So," began Kevin, "does your church use biblical methods for choosing new members?"

No one asked what he meant, but they all turned to face him.

"You know, did they cast lots to see who could join your church?"

CHAPTER 27

Marissa at the Office

Two Months Later

"I THOUGHT THIS WAS A SOCIAL CALL, MARISSA," stated Nattie, "but you look too serious."

"It's about our case," Marissa told her as she dropped into one of the upholstered chairs in Nattie's office.

"Our closed case?"

"Don't worry, it's still closed."

Eyebrows raised, "Still?"

"It's a good-news / bad-news thing. What do you want to hear first?"

"Start with the one that's bigger, then."

Marissa paused to consider Nattie's response and realized, "I guess I've already given you the good news, which is that we have the Ellis and Goldman killer in custody. The bad news is that it isn't the Dobbs brothers."

"I assume you're about to tell me the story."

"We had to cut Lucas and Robert loose on the murder charge because they had an airtight alibi."

"I thought you had discredited their alibi."

"Their first alibi was that they were arranging an engagement for their troupe up in Roanoke. That was a lie. Lucas had made all those arrangements over the phone earlier that day. That alibi was to cover up what they were really doing, which was robbing a pharmacy in Morristown."

"And they'd rather face a robbery charge than a murder charge."

"It'll be more serious than just robbery. They were stealing narcotics to sell. That'll get them some serious time."

"But you said you have the murderer in custody."

"We do. It's a woman named Elaine Claire."

Straining her eyebrows together in an effort to recognize the name, Nattie came up blank.

"That's the woman from the Red Hill case."

"From twenty years ago?"

"Yes. She had been turning tricks around the campgrounds during that race weekend, and she remembers haggling with the Dog Pack guys over how much she was going to charge them. And then she got drugged."

"Rohypnol?"

"Maybe. There's no toxicology report to verify it, but that drug dates back to the early '70s. And she claimed she'd been drugged before and knew what it felt like."

"That hardly seems like it would get a guy a life sentence."

"There's more," Marissa said. "He took her home, stuffed more drugs down her throat, and then nearly beat her to death."

"Mercy."

"The judge said it was the most heinous display of brutality that had ever come before him."

"With an uncle like that, it's no wonder Sunny's got such a distrustful personality. I wonder what he did to her."

"That's a curious thing, though, because with a violent act like this, there's usually a history of violence that precedes it, but this appears to be an isolated event. At least there was no record of anything else that I could find."

"So what about the woman? What was her name again?"

"Elaine Claire. When she was a working girl she called herself 'E'Claire.'"

"Cute," sneered Nattie. "What makes you think she killed those guys?"

"According to her statement back then, she doesn't remember how she got home. A neighbor found her in front of her trailer and called 911. She claimed she was not a drug user but having been drugged before she knew what it felt like. She remembers telling those 'gentlemen' no. Apparently they wanted a group discount, and she was unwilling. According to her they drugged her and did what they pleased with her. Then, when one of them took her home, she started to come out of her stupor and told him she knew what had happened to her. When she threatened to go to the police is when he went off on her."

"So she could identify him," stated Nattie.

Shrugging, "Not exactly. According to E'Claire, Reed Hill was not in the tent with the other men when she got there that night. She could identify most of them, but not him."

"Was there other evidence?"

"Yeah. Pretty strong evidence, too. His was the only DNA on her when they examined her. Also she had the good sense to grab something from the truck while she was still in it. It was Reed Hill's Purple Heart medal. Besides all of that, he confessed."

"Wow, he tried to kill her to avoid a rape charge."

143

"That's what got him the long sentence."

"That answers the 'Why Bristol?' question, but Reed Hill is dead. Why would she kill Herman Ellis and Dick Goldman? And why now after all these years?"

"Of course, doing it here makes sense. This is where she got hurt, but I can't answer any of the other questions. She is still denying the charges, so there's no explanatory statement yet."

"I assume she must still blame all of them for what happened to her."

"That's our theory," confirmed Marissa.

"That still doesn't explain why now after all these years."

"I don't know. Maybe something in her life changed and it all came back. What I know is that she had clear motive."

"What about opportunity?"

"We can confirm that she was here for both races. She stayed at the Holiday Inn in Johnson City. We have her signature on both registration dates."

"Well," said Nattie, "I guess that solves the mystery of the method of execution."

CHAPTER 28

Emma Iverson

"MISS MORELAND?" THE VOICE FROM HER WAITING ROOM was soft and tentative. Nattie did not recognize it.

From her desk she could look straight through her doorway to a curved mirror mounted at the ceiling over Kevin's desk. There was too much distortion in the mirror to discern who called for her, but she at least could tell that it was a lone female. "I'm back here," Nattie called out. "Come on back."

Emma Iverson appeared in the doorway but did not enter. "You must be surprised to see me here, Miss Moreland. I'm sure I'm the last person you expected to see in your office."

That's the truth, thought Nattie, standing up but staying behind her desk. "I wasn't expecting you, but you're welcome. What brings you here, Miss Iverson?"

"The two men who were arrested for those murders—do you know what is going on with them?"

The question seemed odd to Nattie. Instinctively she withheld what she knew and turned the questioning back toward Emma Iverson. "What is going on with them?"

"When we released the final payment to you for your services, it was based upon the case being closed."

"It was closed."

"Yes, it was, but when we made final payment to you, it was based on the assurance that it was the two brothers who had murdered their associates."

"And that was the official position at the time we met at BMS."

"That *was* the official position."

"Yes, that is what I said. It was the official position at that time."

"Then I take that you *are* aware that the official position has changed since that time."

What is this about? wondered Nattie. "I am aware of that," she confessed.

"And I assume you are aware that they have arrested someone else."

"I am. I did not see a need to keep you informed of those details. You hired me to do independent investigation and bring this case to a speedy resolution. I have done what I was hired to do. And frankly, Miss Iverson, your disapproval of hiring me and your obvious resentment toward me is getting beyond tiresome. If you feel there is a problem with my bill, I will be happy to meet with you and your general manager to go over my bill again line by line. But I am not interested in jousting with you any longer."

"I need to hire you," blurted Emma. The words seemed to catch in her throat as they came out.

"Excuse me?" asked Nattie. She had heard what Emma had said perfectly well but needed more time to process it.

"I want to hire you. That is, I want to hire you if I can." Emma's tone and demeanor had shifted from the stiff, critical, upright posture to a more rounded slump. She looked like she might cry or fall over, or both.

"Please," pointing at the chair across from her desk, "have a seat. What do you want to hire me to do?"

Sitting, Emma's stiff posture returned. "Are you sure you could work for me? It wouldn't be a conflict of interest or anything?"

"No, my work for BMS is finished, as you well know. There'd be no conflict of interest unless my work for you compromised or distorted my work for them."

Emma's normal scowl intensified as she knotted her eyebrows even further, narrowed her eyes, and jutted her chin forward.

"You don't look like you believe me. Why don't you tell me what this is about?"

"The woman they arrested for those murders is my sister."

Okay, thought Nattie, *now I'm surprised.*

"She didn't do it. She couldn't have done it. I know it wasn't her."

"Look, Ms. Iverson, I know it must be hard to think about your sister this way, but the police have a pretty good case against her."

"Not true," Emma blurted, "not true at all. The case against my sister is entirely circumstantial."

"If you can offer any evidence that refutes their circumstantial evidence, then you should just take it over to Marissa Ferguson. That's what I'd have to do if I discovered something."

"I was hoping you already had something to take to Detective Ferguson, Ms. Moreland."

"Me?" The statement felt like an accusation. "What would I have?"

Scooting forward to the edge of her chair Emma asked, "Are you or are you not working for my husband?"

"No. At this moment I have no current cases that I'm working on. What makes you think I'm working for your husband?"

"He thinks I'm having an affair. He told me he has hired you and that you are following me."

Raising her eyebrows, "Well, that certainly explains your animosity toward me."

The quivering chin returned to Emma Iverson. "I feel I must owe you an apology, Ms. Moreland. I have treated you unfairly. I'm sorry for my rudeness. I'm so confused. First I resented your presence in my personal life and then in my professional life, and then I was glad for it."

"Glad?"

"Yes. As much as I hated the scrutiny, I had come to think of it as fortuitous. Had you been spying on my husband, you might have been able to provide the alibi my sister needs. The case against her is mostly based upon her having a revenge motive, but it just isn't so. Her life was a mess, but after all that happened she really straightened herself out. She finished college with a nursing degree, now she's working in Nashville and taking care of her family. She and her husband have two teenaged girls. She would do anything to keep all of that stuff buried in the past."

"I believe you, but the case against her isn't just based on motive. That wouldn't be enough to get her arrested. She had opportunity, too. They have pretty strong evidence that she was here for both murders."

"I know," sighed Emma, "and I know why she was here for both murders."

"You do?"

"Yes. You see," Emma looked down and fumbled with her hands, "she was taking care of my son while the race was going on. My son Merrill—he's twenty-four—is quadriplegic. That's why she was always here for the races." Looking up at Nattie, she stopped talking.

Nattie interpreted the look and hesitation as an appeal for her to fill in the missing puzzle pieces. Nattie kept quiet.

"I was having an affair. I am having an affair. It's with a man I went to high school with. We're very discreet. We only meet when my husband is involved with something very big."

"Like the race."

"Yes. And since he doesn't approve of my sister, my children know to keep her presence here a secret."

"So you assumed that I could validate that story and in so doing exonerate your sister, or at least provide another explanation of why she was here those weekends."

"Exactly."

"I'm sorry that I cannot help you, Emma. I truly am. But even without my corroboration you can still tell Detective Ferguson your story."

"I suppose I have to," Emma said as she stood. "I'm sorry to have taken up your time."

Circling the desk, "No apology necessary there, Emma. I'm just glad that I understand our relationship now."

Frowning, Emma stuck out her hand. "I'm sorry about all of that too, Miss Moreland. You deserved to be treated better."

Shaking Emma's hand, "Thank you for that, Emma, and if you don't mind I'd prefer it if you'd call me 'Nattie.'"

In spite of its stiffness their hug felt sincere to Nattie. "I hope things work out for your sister."

CHAPTER 29

"Real Date" with Nathan

"WHERE ARE WE GOING?" ASKED NATTIE AGAIN as Nathan parked his car along the southern side of Market Street.

Chuckling, "Are you keeping count of how many times you have asked me that in the last half hour?"

Looking out of the passenger window of Nathan's Mustang convertible, "I just like to have my bearings."

"You just hate being in a position to depend on someone else."

Nattie turned toward him. Clearly he thought what he had said was cute. *Don't say what you're thinking,* she told herself.

After getting out of the car and crossing the street Nathan pointed to his right. "It's just a couple of blocks this way."

From where they stood Nattie could see Haggle Shop Antiques, where she had her first encounter with Sunny Hill. The memory made her smile as she recalled how infuriated she was at Sunny's obstinacy. It was truly amazing how her affection for Sunny had grown in spite of the fact that her obstinacy had stayed rigidly intact. *Perhaps,* thought Nattie with a smile, *it has something to do with her rescuing me from Lucas Dobbs.*

Nattie was still relishing her thoughts of Sunny as they crossed Broad Street, but then she caught a glimpse of the building where she had visited Trace Noble in his second-floor office. It was over a year ago when she had worked on the Frank Lester case, but the memory made her shudder. Trace Noble had come very close to killing her. Without thinking she took hold of Nathan's hand as they walked.

The gesture brought a smile to Nathan's face, and he squeezed her hand gently. "I haven't actually been here before, but I heard a couple of ladies describe it at Our House, and it sounded like your kind of place."

"Is that it?" Nattie asked, as she spotted the Mustard Seed Café sign.

Nathan nodded.

They were still holding hands when they stopped in front of the Suzanne Barrett Justis Gallery and looked at the painting of a lounging leopard through the window.

The exposed brick walls of the Mustard Seed Café gave the restaurant an old look. Nattie had an affinity for older, restored things, and this place fit the bill. Whatever it had been before did not include a kitchen, which had been added recently and hidden behind a wall enclosure that went two-thirds of the way to the ceiling.

They both ordered a spinach quiche and tomato soup combination and ice water to drink. The water came in a quart-sized Styrofoam cup that Nattie appreciated, for it was a hot day.

"This is nice, isn't it?" Nathan asked as he scanned the room.

"It is," she answered, looking around the dining room. "I didn't know about this place before."

"I don't mean the place," he explained. "I meant us. This is our third date."

Nattie thought for a moment. "Are you sure?"

"Yeah. We had lunch at Jan Mar's and then at Machiavelli's. This is the third."

"What about the trip to Weaverville and the Stoney Knob?"

He closed his eyes and forced a smile. "Okay, it's our fourth date. I was just going to say that we seem to be stuck in a lunch rut."

"I like lunch," she said. "Besides, don't you have to be at Our House most evenings?"

"I'm the owner. If I know we're going to do something in the evening, I can arrange schedules to get away."

"What did you have in mind?"

"I want to make dinner for you."

The grin of satisfaction on his face told her that the shocked look on her face was what he had hoped for. "You want to cook for me?"

"Enchilada casserole."

"Really?" Still surprised, "You have a casserole recipe."

"It's Beau's recipe," he explained. Beau Robinette had run the Our House kitchen for a short period of time. He was a huge man with a huge array of talents that ranged from chef to counseling to wood-working to vigilante. If anyone could teach Nathan how to cook, it would be Beau.

Nattie missed Beau. She was almost sorry she had run him out of town. "Beau's recipe, huh? Have you made it yet, or am I the guinea pig?"

"I've watched Beau make it, and I've eaten it," he confessed.

"I'll trust you," raising both her index fingers, "but I want it to be Kevin hot instead of Beau hot."

"Oh yeah," agreed Nathan. "I can't handle Beau hot either."

"I assume you want to do this at my house?"

"We can do it at the loft if you want, but I can make it and bring it to your house, too. We'll do whatever you want, Nattie."

"My house. I've got a Mexican cornbread recipe I haven't tried yet." Nattie really had no Mexican cornbread recipe. What she had was a cornbread recipe she had made twice. Kevin told her she could add diced-up jalapeño peppers and make it a Mexican cornbread.

Eli Anderson was the source of Nattie's recipe, which was nothing more than the trick of making a double recipe combining a Jiffy cornbread mix with a Jiffy yellow cake mix. Eli was the adolescent whom she had discovered using her home as a refuge, in return for which he left baked goods. Having more money than time to offer her son, Eli's mother had sent him to boarding school. Nattie, having a weakness for men who need mothering, kept in touch with him.

"That sounds good," he told her. "That Irish beer bread you used to make would have been good, too. You know Mexican food and beer go awfully well together."

The reference to alcohol made Nattie flinch, but her response was interrupted by the return of the waitress.

"Two decaf coffees," Nathan told the server, ordering for both of them.

As the waitress cleared their dishes he said, "How about the Wednesday after the race?"

"Okay."

Pleading, he added, "Now I know there are times when you can't help it what happens, but please try to protect that time. I'm going to have to set up a lot of things on my end to make it happen."

"I'll try," she promised weakly, noticing immediately that he had spotted her hesitation.

The silence that followed was awkward as their coffee arrived. Once they had both doctored their coffees he cleared his throat and said, "Be honest with me, Nattie. Why did you agree to that date?"

"Are we being honest now, Nathan?"

"I'm trying here, but I can't tell if you are."

"I'm not the one who destroyed our marriage."

"No, you're not. I did that all by myself."

"Thank you for saying that."

"But I'm not the one who gave up on us."

"There are a lot of ways to give up on a marriage, Nathan. You chose alcohol as your soul mate a long time before I chose to not live with your mistress."

"And now?"

"What do you mean by 'and now'?"

Leaning across the table and lowering his voice, "I never chose alcohol as my soul mate. It was my crutch. I know why it felt to you like I had a mistress, but that is not an accurate picture from my side of the equation."

"Look, Nathan, if this is what we're going to do here, is it really a good idea?"

Ignoring her objection, "But whatever alcohol was to me, it isn't anymore."

"How do I know that? I couldn't tell when you were lying when we were together. Why should I think I could tell now?"

"I can't give you a reason to trust me. I don't have a reason for you to trust me. But I love you, and I've tried to figure out how to live without you, but I can't. I know I don't deserve you. But," he raised his index finger and smiled at her with a beaming expression that always meant he was about to say something he had rehearsed and was proud of, "I didn't deserve you before we got married either, and you married me anyway. I didn't have a drinking problem then—*and,* listen to me, I don't have a drinking problem now."

"Just because you're sober now doesn't mean you don't have a drinking problem."

"That's true if I am an alcoholic, but are you sure I am an alcoholic?"

Squinting her eyes, "What are you saying?"

"I'm saying that for the first year we were apart I tried to be everything I thought you wanted. I went to AA. I was sober."

"You bought a bar!"

"I bought a tavern, but I surrounded myself there with people in recovery. *And* I made that tavern into a successful business."

"Okay. I'll agree to all that. But you said for the first year you did that. What about after the first year?"

"Well, I figured we were on our way to getting back together when you took me home after that big guy knocked me out. I mean, after we spent that week together, it was like we were married again."

"I know. I blame myself for that. The truth is I don't trust myself with you."

"I thought it was me you didn't trust."

"I don't trust you either. But I don't trust myself. I think it's because if I let you in my heart a little, I'm not sure if I could keep you from coming all the way in."

"Nattie," he moaned, "that doesn't make any sense at all. If we're going to be together, then shouldn't we be together all the way?"

"That's just it. I don't know if we are going to be together."

"Is that because you don't know if it will work, or is it because you don't know if you want it to work?"

"This has never, for even a moment, been about whether or not I wanted our marriage to work."

"So what's the problem?"

She stared back at him with knit eyebrows.

Seeing her expression he held his hands up in surrender. "I know. You don't have to say it. I'm the problem."

"I didn't say that. And I don't believe that. If you have turned the corner on this alcohol junk, then it's me that's stuck in the past."

He put both hands on the table. "Well, then, why don't we agree to go forward? We can establish some rules and go as slow as you want."

"Rules? Are you serious? If we could have negotiated rules and stuck with them, we'd still be married."

"Okay. We won't negotiate the rules."

"How will that work?"

"You'll make the rules, and I'll live by them."

"That's not fair to you, and you know it. Eventually you'd resent me, and I wouldn't blame you."

"If it's the only way to get this started, then it's what I want. Besides, I trust you. You won't abuse that or make it last longer than you need to."

But I'm not sure I trust me to make it last long enough. "Okay, how about this? No physical intimacy."

"Ever?"

"Not for a long time."

"Rule number one," he stated, "no sleepovers. Even after Mexican food."

"Rule number two," she continued without acknowledging his attempt at levity, "no more than one date a week."

"Do you need that?"

Scowling, "Are you negotiating with me now?"

"One date per week it is," he said quickly.

"And for now, let's make the dates just for fun."

"I like fun."

"I mean, nothing heavy, okay? Let's just see if we can enjoy each other's company."

"How about a list?" he said.

Nattie's head jerked back slightly, confused by his question, "What?"

"You want to keep it light, right?"

"Right."

"So, let's do one of your lists. That's still what you do to stay alert when you're on an all-night stakeout. What did you call them?"

"All-nighters. And yes. I still make lists."

"So do you have a list going in your head now?"

"Unlikely food combinations that work."

"Peanut butter and jelly. Scrambled eggs and chorizo," he suggested off the top of his head.

She shrugged.

"What's wrong with those?" he asked.

"Those combinations do work, but they aren't unlikely."

Bobbing his head, "So you want combinations that are not supposed to work together, but they do."

"Yes."

"Grapefruit and milk," he said with a smirk.

"Yes," she told him, matching him smirk for smirk. "They work great together. Have you tried them?"

He grinned at her comeback. "Okay, I'll be serious. Where'd you get the idea for this anyway? It sounds like a Kevin idea."

"It does have a Kevin ring to it, doesn't it? But it came from the Steve Hawkins show at WXBQ a while back."

"What did they come up with?"

"Chocolate ice cream and potato chips."

"Okay. Not bad. How about you? What have you come up with so far?"

"Three so far," she said. "Chicken and waffles, Fritos and bananas, and French fries and a Wendy's Frosty."

"Are you kidding? You haven't got peanut butter on your list at all."

"So, go ahead. The peanut butter category is wide open."

"I know you said peanut butter and jelly doesn't count as unlikely, but what if it was pepper jelly? Is that unlikely enough for you?"

"It is. What else you got, peanut-butter boy?"

The jab brought a crooked smile to him. "Popcorn and M&M'S."

"Movie dinner," she said, remembering that popcorn and M&M'S was what he called his standard movie-theater purchase.

"Movie dinner," he repeated. "How about peanut butter and dill pickle?"

"Peanut butter and bread and butter pickles," she countered.

He looked at her with his head turned sideways. "What was that sandwich you used to put bread and butter pickles on?"

"Egg salad," she answered meekly. "I know, weird." Then, pointing at him, she added, "But not as weird as putting hot sauce on chocolate ice cream."

A dreamy look settled on him as he sat silently gazing at her.

"What?" she asked.

"I just miss this," he said. "Playful banter is one of the things I love about you."

She smiled back at him. It was a tender thing he had said, and she knew he was sincere. And she also knew that he did not need to know that her immediate thought was to remember, *Playful banter was the one thing my father did well just before he left us.*

CHAPTER 30

Food City Family Race Night

"Aren't you the detective who came to my mother's house in Weaverville?"

It took Nattie a moment to figure out from where the question came. Nathan's tavern, Our House, was extra crowded because of all the race fans in for the August race, plus all the town folks who came out for the Food City Family Race Night whether they were race fans or not.

"I am," admitted Nattie when she finally made eye contact with Michelle Simmons's daughter, Angie. 'You're Michelle Simmons' daughter, Angie, right? Here for the race?"

"We are in town for the race. My husband is at the hotel out at Exit 7, but I came to be with some old basketball teammates. We were all hoping Pat Summitt would be here. She's starting the race tomorrow. But I was also hoping I'd run into you while I was here," Angie said. "I found your office earlier, but no one was there."

"Yeah, we closed up early today because of all this," she swirled her index finger around at the crowd. "Can I help you with something?"

"I don't think so," said Angie, "but I might be able to help you with something."

"What's that?"

Angie started to answer, but a gong sounded the changing of the hour. It was 7 p.m., which meant that unless there was a sporting event on the overhead televisions, they would be playing the Crosby, Stills, and Nash song "Our House." All the regulars would be singing along with it. There was no way to continue a conversation until the ritual was complete.

Nattie pointed over her shoulder with her thumb and led them outside where the citywide block party was more conducive to talking.

"How's your mom?" asked Nattie when they were finally clear of the noise.

"She's fine. I'm not sure she's found her niche at the nursing home yet, but her health is improving. I think it's because they are regulating her diet. Thanks for asking."

"No problem," said Nattie. "Your mom seemed like a real nice lady."

"Oh," exclaimed Angie, "she is, but I think she lied to you when you were at the house."

I thought so, too, remembered Nattie.

Shuffling slightly to her left, "Actually, I know she lied. I didn't want to say anything because I didn't want to embarrass her, but I knew there was no way she would have thrown away one of Daddy's diaries."

"I wondered about that myself."

"After I got Momma settled in the nursing home, I had to go back to the house to attend to all the possessions she couldn't take with her."

"Including the diaries?"

Angie nodded yes. "I took a huge box of diaries home with me the next day. I think I found out why she lied. I don't know if it has to do with what you were investigating, but I'm almost certain it was what she wanted to keep secret. Are you still working on the same thing?"

"Not really. That case was settled ten weeks ago, but there are still some loose ends. Can you tell me anything about what you discovered?" Nattie asked. "It might make a difference."

"It was something that happened when I was a little girl. I don't remember much about it, but I think it's why we moved from Kingsport to Weaverville." She looked around before she continued in a lower voice. "Do you know about the man who went to prison?"

"Reed Hill?"

"He was framed."

CHAPTER 31

Waiting

ANGIE AGREED TO BRING THE BOX OF HER FATHER'S DIARIES to Nattie's office when her husband returned to pick her up. The diaries were in the back of their car.

Angie went back into the Our House Tavern to join some former basketball teammates, so Nattie had some time to kill.

One of the nice things about the location of the Natasha McMorales Agency office location was its proximity to State Street and all the activities that include blocking off sections of the street—the Rhythm & Roots music festival, the summer Border Bashes, and the Food City Family Race Night. It afforded Nattie an easy place to get away when she got peopled out, and a place to store rather than carry things like her camera bag or lawn chairs.

Although she was anxious to dive into Ike's journals, she had plenty of time to stroll back to her office at a leisurely pace from Our House. She stopped at the kettle corn trailer and bought a small bag of the caramel corn. A street festival was not complete without at least a small bag of caramel kettle corn. The plan was to return to the office before she opened the bag. If she opened it on the street there was a very good chance she would finish it off and be tempted to get a bag of the plain. Unfortunately the plan failed immediately because as she walked she heard Megan Jean and KFB playing on a small stage near Shanghai's Chinese Buffet. The music reminded her of what she had heard the year before while on a case in New Orleans. By the time Megan Jean had finished singing "These Bones," Nattie realized she had heard it before. Kevin had shown her a YouTube video of it that had been filmed in front of the King Building on Shelby Street. By the time the song was over she also realized the kettle corn bag was empty, and she regretted having opened it at all.

Five minutes later she fell backward into the upholstered chair across from her desk. Looking at her watch she reckoned she had ten minutes to relax in peace. Closing her eyes she said "Peace and good-will" aloud, using the Saint Francis greeting to creation.

Of course, she said to herself, looking at the ringing phone, *the minute I appreciate the solitude, you ring.* "This is Nattie," she said into the receiver.

"Hi, Nattie, this is Angie. I'm at my hotel now, but my brother-in-law just showed up, and he'll only be here for a while. Can I bring these journals to your office when we take him back to his campsite?"

"Oh sure," said Nattie, "but I don't mind coming to your hotel to get them either."

"Ahh," hesitated Angie.

"If it's more convenient for you to bring it by later, that's fine, too. There's a mail slot in my door if I'm not here, but I might still be here."

"Thanks, I'll be by there later."

It was 8:30 p.m. when she lay down on the couch in her waiting room and began reading *The Help.* It was just past midnight and the book was lying on the floor next to her when the phone started ringing. She stepped on it on her way to her office.

"Id dis Nadasha?"

Oh great, she sighed, *a drunk with a phone.* "Yes, it is. How can I help you?"

Nattie listened to his heavy breathing for only a moment before she decided to hang up. Before she could actually hang up, though, the man tried to speak. "Id da bownie."

After listening to thirty seconds of silence Nattie sarcastically said, "Thanks for sharing." Hearing no response from the other end she added, "Enjoy the brownie, sir," and hung up.

Before she took her eyes off the phone it rang again. "Listen, sir," she barked, "do not call here again."

"Nattie?" It was Marissa's voice. "Are you okay?"

Long sigh, "I'm sorry Marissa, I didn't mean to bite your head off. I just got off the phone with a drunk looking for a phone date."

"That's alright. I was just going by your office, when I saw the light on I wondered how you were doing."

"I'm fine. I just ran into the daughter of the Dog Pack Corporal who kept all the records. She's going to bring them by in a few minutes."

"Let me know if it turns up anything interesting."

"Of course. She says Reed Hill was framed."

"I don't see how that's possible," said Marissa. "Framing him would be quite a trick."

"Why do you say that?"

"We looked at that case again pretty thoroughly when we were indicting Elaine Claire. Reed Hill's DNA was all over her."

"Speaking of E'Claire, how did the alibi with her sister check out?"

"We checked into it, but it wasn't going to clear her of the charges. She was with her sister's kids until ten o'clock. That still gave her plenty of time to get over to the Speedway and settle her score."

The picture of a disappointed Emma Iverson passed through Nattie's awareness and lingered until the sound of Angie coming through the door broke her trance. "Thanks for trying, Marissa. I need to go. My delivery just got here."

"I hope you're talking about reading material and not that drunk looking for a phone date."

CHAPTER 32

Sportsman's Bar

"Meet you where?" asked Marissa. It was two in the morning. The extra duty required by the influx of so many race fans meant that Marissa had not slept the night before. The exhaustion showed in her voice.

"Sportsman's Bar," repeated Nattie. "You know where it is, don't you?"

"Of course, but what's this about, Nattie?"

"I'm pretty sure another murder is happening right now."

Nattie entered the bar by herself. The music was loud and the male-dominated clientele louder. If she had to guess she would have said the average age of the men in the bar was in the neighborhood of fifty-five. The few women in the place were closer to forty. No one paid much attention to her as she wound her way through the crowd looking for one of the Dog Pack guys. Although Denny Hamlin had won the race earlier most of the buzz was on the clash between Tony Stewart and Matt Kenseth. The consensus was that Stewart had used his helmet to throw a prefect strike into the front grill of the Kenseth car.

"Hey, look, Lurch. It's Natasha," she heard Grey Troutman's nasally voice to her left. "Over here, sugar," he called out.

As she made her way toward them, she had to pass between two clusters of younger men. A bodybuilder in a muscle shirt to her left stepped into her path as she tried to squeeze by. "Where are you going?" he asked, after which he looked back to his friends with a cat-like grin on his face.

Come on, junior, I don't need this now. "I'd just like to pass by, if you don't mind," she said with as much politeness as she could muster under the circumstances. If another request was necessary, it would be more forceful.

Still looking at his friends he said, "And I'd just like an answer to my question, if you don't mind."

"If she doesn't mind, I do" came Larry Yarborough's booming voice from what to the bodybuilder must have seemed like right above his head.

Startled, the bodybuilder turned quickly, but Larry had positioned his huge body so close behind him that his turning produced a momentary bump between his right shoulder and Larry's midsection. Larry timed the bump with a shove of his stomach that bounced the younger man away like a rag doll.

Not waiting for the bodybuilder to collect himself, Larry once again crowded him so that his voice was directly over the younger man's head. "She asked you to let her pass. What's your answer gonna be, sport?"

"I'd let her pass if I were you, Opie," chided Grey from the booth where he and Larry had been sitting.

"I was just having a little fun," said the bodybuilder, motioning for Nattie to pass with his left arm. He was no longer looking at Larry.

As the group left, one of the bodybuilder's friends gave Grey a menacing look, to which Grey responded by laughing out loud.

"Where's Ozzie?" asked Nattie before Larry could sit back down.

"What do you want him for? We're the ones who just saved you."

"What do you mean 'we'?" asked Larry.

"Thank you, Larry, but this is important, really. Where is Ozzie?" she asked more frantically.

"He's counting the money with Sunny," answered Larry.

"He should be here anytime now, though," added Grey. "We only had two tents here this trip."

"Come with me," Nattie demanded. She turned sideways and nudged her head toward the door. "Show me where they are."

Larry led the way out immediately, parting the crowd like the Red Sea.

"What's this about?" asked Grey, still sitting in spite of the fact that Larry was already disappearing through the crowd.

Over her shoulder she said, "I think she's going to kill Ozzie next," as she followed Larry out.

"Shee-it!" exclaimed Grey as he scrambled up and began hurrying to catch up.

"Unbelievable," moaned Nattie, following Grey out into the dark parking lot.

Larry, standing in the middle of the parking lot with his hands held up and out, faced the door of the bar. Between Larry and Nattie were the bodybuilder and his three friends. The one who had given Grey the dirty look was holding a gun.

"Lower your gun now or die," said Nattie with an exaggerated slowness. She gripped the gunman's collar from behind and held the nuzzle of her Smith and Weston .38 against the back of his head.

The gun was slowly lowered as the other three friends moved away, staring wide-eyed at Nattie.

Taking the gun from the lowered hand, Grey said, "You don't really want no trouble, do you, young fella?"

"What's going on here?" yelled Marissa, approaching the gathering from around the corner. Her gun was drawn, and she held it out with both hands.

"Are you okay, Nattie?"

Shoving the gunman toward his friends, "We are. Thanks for coming. We've got to get over to the Speedway, though."

Marissa's gun was still pointed at the four assailants. "You boys go on back inside now."

"What about his gun?" asked one of the gunman's friends.

With Marissa's arrival Grey had immediately pocketed the gun. When the question of the gun was asked, he looked around as if it might be lying on the asphalt somewhere.

"I'd suggest you consider yourself lucky that I don't have time to mess with your question," said Marissa, staring at them, "because if I did you'd be looking at a charge of brandishing a firearm. So I'd suggest you go back inside *now.*"

Waiting until they were inside and the door was shut, Marissa holstered her weapon. Holding her hand out to Grey, "I'll take the handgun, please."

"I was just waiting for the right time to give it to you," Grey said, handing her the gun.

"Let's go," said a frustrated Larry. "Ozzie's in trouble."

Pointing at Grey, Marissa said, "You come with me and show me where we're going." To the others she added, "I'll lead. You two follow me."

Larry had to sit sideways in the back of Nattie's Subaru Forester. Nattie followed Marissa, who had her lights on in spite of the fact that there was virtually no traffic. As they entered the campsite she turned on her siren.

Stopping in front of a small camper Marissa jumped from her car with her gun drawn. She stopped long enough to point at the tent to the left of the camper.

"Sunny," Marissa called out, "this is Bristol Police. Please come out with your hands in the air."

There was no response. Marissa motioned for Grey and Larry to stay in their respective places, then pointing two fingers at her own eyes and then the front of the tent, she told Nattie to watch the tent.

Positioning herself on the far side of the tent opening, Nattie could watch both the tent and Marissa's approach to the camper.

"I repeat," stated Marissa firmly as she stood directly in front of and five feet from the closed door, "this is the Bristol Police. Come out slowly with your hands in the air."

Hearing and seeing no response, Marissa moved to the side of the camper. She slung the door open with her left hand as her right hand pointed her weapon through the doorway into the right end of the camper. Still nothing moved. With her gun still aiming into the open door, she slowly circled the open doorway until she could see into the left side of the camper.

"I got him," Marissa called out as she disappeared inside.

The absence of fear in Marissa's declaration let them all know that Ozzie Applewhite was still alive. Neither Grey nor Larry had obeyed the command to stay in the cars. Each was standing behind the car they were told to stay in, and each was anxiously waiting for something to do. Marissa's words brought them both running toward the camper.

Nattie also was relieved by the tone of Marissa's voice. Anxious to join the others, she crossed in front of the tent opening, immediately realizing her mistake. Sunny Hill, who had been watching everything from inside the tent, rushed out behind her and began sprinting in the opposite direction.

Giving chase was all Nattie could do as Sunny stayed steadily ahead of her. Crossing the four-lane highway first, Sunny stopped and turned to face Nattie, who was still on the other side. The two women stared at each other across the empty road. The look on Sunny's face was not what Nattie would have expected in such a moment. There was no fear of being caught or hatred for being an enemy, but a sad look of betrayal. She had the look of a little girl whose birthday cake had just been dropped.

"Stay right there," yelled Nattie, pointing the gun across the road.

Staring back, Sunny pursed her lips together and slowly shook her head back and forth. They stood like that until the sound of a car distracted them. The car was on Nattie's side of the road, and as soon as it neared Nattie, Sunny turned and continued running into the chaos that still surrounded the racetrack.

Once the car passed, Nattie lined up a shot with her gun, exhaled slowly, and then lowered the gun to her side.

CHAPTER 33

Ozzie Applewhite's Story

THERE WAS NO TELLING HOW MUCH LONGER Ozzie had to live had they not intervened. Nattie was thankful she missed the scene while she was chasing Sunny, but it was clear from their comments that Ozzie was in the same condition Herman Ellis and Dick Goldman had been in before they died. He was stripped naked and bound to a chair with his mouth taped shut. He was drugged, but he had not been cut.

By the time Nattie returned to the camper, Ozzie had his clothes on. He was sitting in a camp chair, with his head drooping to one side and his hands folded in his lap.

Larry and Grey, who were huddling around their friend, both turned to watch Nattie's approach. Ozzie turned as well, but the slowness of his reaction and the clumsiness of his movement told Nattie that he was still under some effects of being drugged.

Marissa, on her cell phone, stood next to her car and gave Nattie a thumbs-up. When she closed her phone she said, "There's a patrol car picking her up right now."

"Really," Nattie said. "That was quick."

Pointing at Grey, "We got a good description of her from this gentleman. They were on her as soon as she got to BMS."

"That's Grey Troutman," Grey informed her, slowly pronouncing his name, "in case you need it for your report."

That being settled, Nattie turned her attention to Ozzie. "How's he doing?"

"He's been drugged. It was probably Rohypnol, like the others, but we won't know that for a while. EMTs are on the way just to check him out."

Kneeling down in front of Ozzie, Nattie asked, "How are you feeling?"

"Neber bebber," Ozzie slurred.

That's a good sign, Nattie smiled.

"It duz in da bownie," he told her.

So you were my drunk caller, Nattie realized. Turning toward Marissa, "I think you might want to hear this."

As Marissa came to stand behind Nattie, Grey translated, "He said, 'It was in the brownie.'"

Marissa asked Ozzie, "Is that true? Did she drug you with a brownie?"

"Des," Ozzie said, nodding slowly.

"That's probably what she did with Herm and Dick, too," observed Larry.

"Yeah," agreed Grey, "that's why we saw each of them after they finished counting. She gave them one of her famous brownies. She knew they wouldn't eat it 'til they got home. You had to have something to drink with it to get down all that sweet."

"Whose camper is this?" asked Marissa.

"Ozzie's," answered Larry.

"So when they finished counting, she sent him home with one of her special brownies," surmised Nattie, "and then she waited until it did its work." To Ozzie she asked, "Do you remember anything about eating the brownie or her taking your clothes off?"

Ozzie shook his head no.

"She'd remember it if it was me she stripped down," Grey said as he puffed his chest out and hiked up his pants.

"E bamed us por Bed," slurred Ozzie.

"She blamed you for what happened to Reed Hill?" repeated Marissa.

"Des."

"Why did she blame you for what happened to Reed Hill?" asked Marissa.

"I think I can explain that," said Nattie. "I have Ike Simmons's diary from back then. It's a detailed account of that whole affair."

"I'm going to need that," said Marissa.

"I'll get to you later this morning."

"Is that how you figured out that it was Sunny?"

"It is."

They all turned in unison toward the road. The sound of the approaching ambulance blipped as they entered the campsite area.

Turning back to Ozzie, Marissa pointed at Nattie. "I think you should know, sir, that Miss Moreland here just saved your life."

Nattie blushed. Marissa grinned.

Ozzie smiled a crooked smile and slurred, "Dank ou Nadasha."

After checking Ozzie's vitals the medics pronounced him stable, but they were still taking him to the hospital for a precautionary night of observation.

Marissa followed the ambulance to the hospital, leaving Nattie and the two remaining Dogs to tend to the campsite. Silently they went about the business of locking up the camper and closing up the tent.

Just before climbing into Nattie's car, Grey broke the silence. "You know, it's funny," he said. "Those were really great brownies. They'd have been great all by themselves, but she used to put different candy

bar pieces inside them. You'd take a bite, and it would be mint chocolate chips and the next bite could be caramel or peanuts."

"I liked the Peppermint Pattie ones," added Larry.

"I don't get it," said Nattie. "What's so funny about that?"

"It's just that Corporal Ike used to say that Sunny's brownies were
'to die for.'"

CHAPTER 34

The Bristol, TN Jail

"Do you want to talk to her?" asked Marissa. Nattie had just handed her Ike Simmons's diary.

"Can I?" asked a surprised Nattie. She had not expected to have the option to speak to Sunny now that she was in custody, so the question had not crossed her mind.

"You might as well," answered Marissa. "That will give me time to check out the diary before you go. Besides, she asked for you."

"What does she want with me?"

"She knows it was you who read the diary."

"She knows about the diary?" asked Nattie.

Marissa nodded her head up and down. "I think she's got some questions about what's in it."

"Is there anything I need to avoid talking about? I don't want to say anything that will interfere with your case."

"That's not an issue at this point. She confessed to everything. It's a good confession. She gave us details only the killer would have known."

"Wow, she opened up?"

"I wouldn't say she opened up. She described what she did to those men as if she was giving directions to Ridgewood Barbecue."

The door to the interview room opened, and Sunny came into view. She appeared to be listening to whomever was to her left and beyond Nattie's field of vision. Sunny nodded her head once, stepped into the room, and the door closed behind her. It was not until the door closed that she made eye contact with Nattie, and then it was an unflinching stare. In the oversized jumpsuit provided by the jail, Sunny looked more like a little girl than she did in the halter-top and skin-tight blue jeans she usually wore. Her hair was in a ponytail that looked like it had been unraveling all night.

Sitting down on the other side of the small table from Nattie, Sunny asked, "Why didn't you shoot me?"

"I didn't want to shoot you, Sunny. I just wanted to stop you."

Sunny put her forearms on the table, turned her head to the left, and snorted, "You'd-a had to shoot me to stop me if they hadn't have got me."

Nattie waited for her to turn back.

"It was only a matter of time before they got you."

"I don't care nothing about that. I just didn't get to finish."

"Was it worth it?" Nattie asked.

"If I'd-a finished, it would be."

And now you're going to spend the rest of your life behind bars, thought Nattie.

"That cop said you were the one who figured out that it was me. Is that true?"

"Yes."

"She said you read Mr. Simmons's diary."

"That's true."

Looking down, Sunny's voice got softer and weaker. "Would you tell me?"

Pulling her chair closer to the table, Nattie mirrored Sunny's arms and elbows on the table and stooped closer.

Sunny stared at her again. Her right eye twitched. She half-asked, half-stated, "You read about what happened to my uncle Reed?"

"I did."

"If you don't mind, that's what I want to hear about."

Nattie took a long, slow breath and began the story. "It happened on a Pack and Play night. I know you know what that means." Pausing, Nattie waited for a sign of recognition on Sunny's face.

Seeing nothing but an unwavering stare, Nattie continued. She had Sunny's undivided attention, but she had no idea what was going in Sunny's head. "Ike Simmons and your uncle Reed were doing the counting that night. The rest of the Dog Pack were playing poker when they were visited by a prostitute."

"She's the one they arrested," observed Sunny.

"Yes, Elaine Claire."

"I felt bad about that, but she'd-a got let go after the last race."

You mean after you killed Ozzie, thought Nattie. "They argued with her about the charge. I got the impression that it was not the first time they had done business with her. She wanted $75, and they wanted to give her $150 for a group deal. I think it was Mr. Dobbs, that's Lucas and Bobby's father, right?"

"Yeah."

"When he didn't get what he wanted, he just drugged her and took what he wanted."

"Uncle Reed wasn't there," Sunny stated tentatively.

"He wasn't there then."

"Not then, no."

"They said he raped her and then drove her out into the middle of nowhere and tried to beat her to death," Sunny told her.

"I know."

"But it wasn't true. I always believed it. I didn't want to believe it, but I did."

"If you always believed he did it, then why did you start blaming the other men?"

"I got a letter. Actually what I got was a letter and one of those Mr. Simmons diaries. It began with me taking Uncle Reed's place in the Dog Pack and how Mr. Simmons taught me to take his place as the money man."

That explains the missing volume, realized Nattie. She had not noticed that a book was missing the night before, because as soon as she read the preceding volume she knew she had to hurry to the Speedway. The missing volume became evident this morning when Nattie was deciding what volumes to bring to Detective Ferguson. "I didn't see that diary. What did it say about your uncle being framed?"

"Nothing," answered Sunny, "but there was a letter, too. It said Uncle Reed and Mr. Simmons were not part of what happened to that woman, but the rest of them were."

"And when you got that letter, is that when you decided to kill them?"

"Yeah."

"I'm just curious, Sunny, was the letter from North Carolina?"

"Yeah. Weaverville, North Carolina."

"Do you know who it was from?"

"It didn't say, but I always figured it was Mr. Simmons's wife."

"Did you try to follow up with her?"

"I didn't see no reason to."

"Can you remember the exact wording on that letter?"

"Why?" she asked coldly.

Like I said, "I'm just curious."

Sunny's eyes drifted up and to the left. "The letter said that since Old Man Dobbs was dead, I should know Uncle Reed didn't do what they said he did. It said all but two of them men raped that woman, and it said that he and Mr. Simmons were counting the money when it was happening. It was Dobbs who took her home in Uncle Reed's truck. That's why he got blamed. It said Dobbs threatened to hurt me, and that's why Uncle Reed never spoke up for himself."

Nattie sat quietly and let what she had heard sink in.

"I do have one regret," Sunny continued.

Coming without provocation, the comment struck Nattie as odd. "What's that?"

In a matter-of-fact tone, she said, "I wish Old Man Dobbs would have lived long enough for me to have kilt him." Tilting her head to the right, she asked, "Why were you curious about them words?"

Nattie sighed, "There was a reason why Mrs. Simmons said that stuff in a letter. She didn't want to send you the diary with the information about that night, so she sent you the other diary. She knew you'd be interested in that one."

"Why didn't she want to send the other one?"

"She was protecting her husband. You see, your uncle and Ike Simmons weren't there when it all began, but they got there late." She paused again to watch Sunny, but still there was nothing in her expression to belie what she was thinking. "According to the diary, when they got there Miss E'Claire was still there. They flipped a coin and Mr. Simmons won, so he got to be with her next. When it was your uncle's turn there were no more condoms, so he left DNA evidence."

"He was guilty," she stated without a blink.

"He was guilty of being with her while she was drugged. That's probably why he kept quiet about everything else."

"Because he was going to do time anyway."

"Yes."

"But he's not the one who beat her up, is he?"

"No, that was Louis Dobbs. He used your uncle's truck to take her home. Later he told Mr. Simmons that she knew she had been drugged and raped. She threatened to go to the police. That's when he tried to kill her. Luckily for her, he gave her too many drugs, and she threw up."

"Did he threaten Uncle Reed with me?" She looked sad, finally.

"Mr. Simmons and your uncle were the only ones who were threatened to keep quiet. They were the only ones who knew the whole story. I think the rest of them suspected something wasn't right. Dick Goldman's wife said it changed him."

"The letter said that there were two of them men that didn't touch that woman."

It was the question she dreaded. "Ozzie Applewhite was not part of the assault on her. He left when she first got there."

Nattie let that information sink in.

Sunny Hill had almost killed an innocent man. Nattie watched her closely but saw no change in her face other than she was now staring at the wall to her left. The biggest effect was on her shoulders. She appeared to be holding her breath. "I sure didn't want to hurt nobody that didn't deserve it."

"I believe you," said Nattie softly.

Turning back to Nattie, "Who was the other one?"

Nattie looked hard into Sunny's eyes. The hard, defiant look was still there, but somewhere deeper yet was a little girl who, much like Nattie, had to grow up long before she could be grown up, a little girl with a child's sense of loyalty and justice.

"The other man was Larry Yarborough," lied Nattie. Sunny didn't need to know that Dick Goldman was the other innocent man.

Standing slowly, Sunny took a deep breath. "I'd-a guessed it was him." She walked over to the door and knocked twice.

"Will you do me one favor, Miss Moreland?" she asked as the door opened behind her.

"Sure, Sunny. What do you want me to do?"

"Tell Mr. Applewhite I'm sorry."

CHAPTER 35

Manna Bagel

"YOUR FRIEND WAS JUST HERE," SAID MARISSA, putting down her book as Nattie entered Manna Bagel. She was sitting in the window seat to the left of the door. She liked to sit facing State Street. It gave her a good view of outside. A single cup of coffee was perched on the table in front of her.

"Debbie?"

"Yes. Is she okay?"

"What do you mean?"

"She recognized me when she came in, so we shared a cup of coffee together. I'll bet she was only here for five minutes before her husband tracked her down."

"Yeah," agreed Nattie, "that happens a lot. He's kind of controlling."

Raising her right eyebrow, "I hope that's all it is."

"What do you mean?" asked Nattie.

"I don't know. It's probably doesn't mean anything." Marissa flipped her hand over, trying to dismiss the subject. Standing, she added, "I need more coffee. Are you getting anything?"

"Yes, but I'm not sure what. Are you eating?"

"I had a wrap. I'm just nursing coffee now, but please, get something and join me."

While Marissa refilled her coffee cup at the urn, Nattie ordered the tomato bisque soup and a spinach-feta cheese bagel. By the time Nattie returned with her Sierra Mist from the fountain, Marissa had stashed her book away. Nattie took the seat across from her, putting her back toward the street. "Okay, now come on. Tell me."

"Tell you what, Nattie?"

"Tell me what you meant about Debbie's husband."

"I probably shouldn't have said anything." She contorted her face. "Just forget I said it."

"Come on, what are you thinking? You think she's being abused, don't you?"

"No," Marissa moaned. But then her voice got deeper. "Well, maybe not, but she's well on her way to Battered Woman's Syndrome."

"So you *do* think she's being abused."

"Not necessarily. There are different kinds of abuse, and they all come in varying degrees of violation."

After thinking a moment, Nattie shook her head. "Debbie's not abused. Her husband's a pig."

"A controlling pig," amended Marissa.

"Yeah, but he's never hit her."

"How do you know?"

"She would have told me."

"Would she?"

Nattie thought for another moment. "Yes, I think she would have told me. Are you saying she wouldn't?"

"I don't presume to know her better than you do. I've met her twice, and both times she defended him."

"She's protective," explained Nattie.

"Maybe, but her protection, as you call it, came without provocation both times."

Nattie knew there was a concerned look on her face, but she could not help it.

"Look, I just listened to her on the phone with him, and in a matter of a minute the conversation went from her telling him how she felt about something he did, to her apologizing for feeling that way and making him feel guilty for what he had done. Then she got off the phone and defended his right to be angry with her about it."

"I don't know, Marissa. That sounded pretty bad the way you described it." Shrugging, "If you didn't add the anger part at the end, it sounded a lot like most of the conversations with men I've ever had."

"Maybe, but there's a big difference between being over-responsible for the men in your life and accepting blame for their shortcomings."

"And you think Debbie's doing that?"

"Yes."

"And that's a bad sign?"

"Yes."

"And my food is here," Nattie declared, as she spotted Carol walking toward them with her soup. *Not Debbie,* Nattie told herself as Carol put her plate on the table in front of her.

"Have you read *In Your Father's Eyes?*" asked Marissa, as Nattie put Shed Spread on her bagel.

"No, is it a mystery?"

Smirking, "Cops don't read mysteries. It's sort of a psychological book." She dug the book out and held it up.

"Asoph Saylor," exclaimed Nattie, pointing at the cover. "He wrote—"

"The Real McGoo," they said in unison.

"I met him a year ago when I was in New Orleans."

"Wow, it is a small world—after all," Marissa clenched her teeth together in an effort to apologize for the joke.

"Have you read *The Real McGoo?*" asked Nattie.

"Not yet. A friend of mine from grad school sent me both books last week. She said he's getting to be a favorite author with social workers. I'll read it next."

"I'm sure you'll love it. I did."

"What did you think of him?" asked Marissa.

Nattie smiled warmly as she remembered the author. "It's funny that you ask me that while you're holding that book, because what I remember most about him is the twinkle in his eyes."

"The twinkle?"

Nattie laughed. "You know, the kind of eye-smile your grandfather would have when he'd watch you figure something out as a child."

"That is amazing," observed Marissa. "That's kind of what this book is about."

"Really?"

"You know how we all crave hearing our father say he's proud of us? Well, it's based on that idea. We all want to see in our mother's eyes that we are loved, no matter what we do. And in our father's eyes, we want to see that what we do matters."

With her mouth full of soup, Nattie could only nod her head to say that she was following what Marissa was saying.

"So this book," tapping on the cover, "is written to people who didn't get to see their father's blessings in his eyes. Maybe he was already gone when they were old enough for his blessing to matter, or maybe he was too wounded or immature himself to give what his children should have gotten."

"What about those children?" asked Nattie, dabbing soup from her mouth. She had already begun wondering if her fascination with twinkling eyes was her own search to substitute for her missing-in-action father. For as long as she could remember, her highest compliment about a man was "He has a twinkle in his eye." Very few men reached that level of esteem.

"I'm not completely finished yet," continued Marissa. "You can borrow it when I'm done. But in a nutshell he says if you know you didn't get your father's blessings because of his inadequacies, then you can capture the look in the eyes of anyone who ever believed in you or encouraged you. The trick is that you have to believe you deserved it in order for you to go get it and claim it for yourself."

"That's quite a trick sometimes."

"Maybe all the time," agreed Marissa, then abruptly she sat up straight and strained to look at something out of the window. "Oh, come on, Doug," she asserted under her breath as she stood. "You know better than that" was the last thing Nattie heard as Marissa rushed through the door.

Nattie watched as she darted across the street toward the open parking lot where a man and woman were arguing. They turned to face Marissa as she approached. The woman leaned away from the man, who held her right elbow in his grip. As Marissa got close to them, the woman pulled away and disappeared around the side of the building. The man disappeared behind Marissa as she got closer to him. Noting that Marissa's gun remained holstered at her side, Nattie decided that this was a routine event in the life of her friend. She was just about to shift her attention back to her soup when Marissa collapsed.

Nattie froze as she watched her friend crumble to the ground. When her disbelief finally subsided, she made a mad dash across the street. She never heard the car brakes screech or the name the driver yelled at her through his window.

CHAPTER 36

Dinner With Nathan

NORMALLY HE WOULD NOT HAVE NOTICED. Normally she could control her emotions well enough so that no one would notice. But something about this was not normal. He noticed.

Maybe it was because she was changing, growing. *That couldn't be it,* she decided. Maybe she had stronger feelings than she had thought. *That could be.*

Or maybe the scene in the movie they were watching had caught her off guard. *Bingo,* she thought, *that's it.*

Up to that point the evening had gone smoothly. Nattie had spent the afternoon cleaning her home and prepping a vegetable-polenta casserole. She needed the afternoon's distraction to forget what had happened the day before. She had stayed awake all night not thinking about it.

The casserole recipe she used came from the Delia Davenport cookbook that Nathan had given her during their engagement. It was by far the most complicated recipe she had ever tried, but it worked. She knew it worked because he had two large helpings and he never would have seconds on vegetables.

They had beer with dinner. One beer each. The question of whether he was an alcoholic or not had lessened in intensity to the point that she thought she would surprise him with "one beer" because it went so well with Mexican food. Kevin told her that Inari Wines would sell single beers and would also help her pick them out. He was right. As Nattie entered the shop, she was greeted by Stan Barringer, who recommended a Statan ale and a Java Head Troeggs dark beer. Nathan had the Java Head with dinner. He closed his eyes and moaned with his first taste. *Thanks Stan,* thought Nattie as she watched him savor it.

The meal had been perfect. Afterward he made a fire in the fireplace while she cleaned up and brewed a pot of decaf coffee. They sat on the couch enjoying bowls of Cappachiano Crunch ice cream from Bristol Eats & Treats while watching the fire. This time, too, was perfect. Even the silence during dessert had seemed natural, even serene.

While Nattie put their dessert dishes in the sink, Nathan put *Pursuit of Happiness* in the DVD player. Neither noticed that the pot of coffee had remained untouched. When the movie started, Nattie took her shoes off and leaned in to Nathan as she lounged on the couch. Before long she was nestled under his left arm with her head resting on his chest. Although he was a good eight inches taller than she was, she always thought their bodies fit together quite nicely in this position. She pulled his left arm around her middle, resting her left arm on top of his.

It all felt very comfortable and natural to her until the bathroom scene came up.

"What happened?" asked Nathan, stopping the movie.

"What do you mean?"

"Come on, Nattie. I could feel you trembling. What happened? Is it about what happened yesterday?"

I don't want to go there now. "No, I'm just real tired, I think," she said.

He leaned forward and held her chin up so he could look directly into her eyes. "You can talk to me, you know."

She searched his eyes, but because she was so close, she had to do it one eye at a time. *I don't even know what I'm looking for.* But she did know what she was looking for. She was looking for a reason not to talk. Not knowing what it looked like, she resorted to her standard response: "I'm okay, really."

She could find no fault in the suspicious expression that slowly emerged on his face. "Let's just watch the movie." She did not believe herself either. "Maybe I'll talk about it tomorrow," she conceded. *Maybe not.*

When he kissed her she could taste salt, which surprised her because at the most she was aware of one or two tears escaping her control. If he noticed he did not know what it meant, so he settled back, wiggled closer under her head, and restarted the movie.

Clenching her jaw and squinting her eyes kept her emotions at bay, but did nothing to stop the pictures from rolling through her awareness. . . .

"Somebody call 911, NOW!" she screamed more authoritatively than she had ever spoken before. Desperation trumped self-consciousness.

Each of the half dozen folks who had gathered around them began fumbling with their cell phones, allowing her to tend to other business. From across the street it had looked like the little man had punched her in the stomach, doubling her over immediately. Nattie had yelled something at him, she could not recall what, as she sprinted to her friend's aid. It was not until she knelt beside Marissa that she noticed the dark red stain on the asphalt. That is when she yelled for help. That being done, it was time to turn her attention to where the blood was coming from.

Marissa was curled up on her side as Nattie knelt behind her. Marissa was holding her stomach and struggling to breathe. Unwrapping the scarf from around her neck, Nattie gently lifted Marissa's hand

and pressed it against the wound. Nattie gasped as she noticed how drenched with blood Marissa's hand was. For a moment, or longer, her memory was failing her as she tried to recall how much time anything took; she was only aware of how she felt. She did not know it at the time, but this shift in focus away from her friend in need would be one of the many guilts that would haunt her sleeplessness. But at the time she was keenly aware of being sick. Dizziness moved from the top of her head downward, and as soon as it passed, a wave of nausea rose upward from her stomach, setting a chill in her neck and head. Determining not to throw up, she tried to swallow, but could not.

Nattie bit the inside of her lip. The memory was too painful to let it continue. She stared at the fire, which had diminished from the roaring blaze it had been when all the newspapers were wadded up under it to a kitchen-burner-sized flame. Nathan never understood that lying logs neatly next to each other made a good stack but choked the oxygen off of a fire.

Removing his arm from around her waist, she sat up.

"What's the matter?" he asked.

"Nothing," she said, trying to make the words sound natural. Patting his shoulder, "I'm just gonna get the fire going again."

Moving his arm farther out of her way, he wiggled back into a better posture and watched her tend to the fire.

Poking at the larger logs was all it took to get more air circulating, and soon the fire was blazing again. She stood in front of the fireplace and watched it glow. Then she held her palms to the heat and immediately wondered why she had done so.

Turning around, she discovered that Nathan had paused the movie and was watching her intently. His clear concern for her at the moment was a momentary comfort, but it quickly transformed into something that felt like a threat. Without further thought she said, "You didn't have to stop the movie."

With an awkward smile, as if he was slightly embarrassed to receive what he thought was a compliment, "Sure I did."

Forcing a smile, "Well, thank you." She knelt beside him on the couch and kissed him quickly before sliding around next to him, snuggling into the same position they had been in before she tended the fire. "Start the movie."

He did not start the movie, though. She could feel his eyes on her. Patting him on the leg, "Really, Nathan, it's okay. Start the movie."

He did not push "play" until she had completely stopped squirming.

Again she determined to keep her emotions at bay. This time she focused her attention intently on the movie. On the screen Will Smith was doing something at a computer terminal. She had missed too much of the movie to know what, but she did notice for the first time that he was wearing glasses. *That just doesn't look right.*

A siren went off outside and startled her, causing her to push off of Nathan's midsection with her elbow.

"What are you doing?" he yelped, rubbing the spot. "It's just a cop outside."

"I'm sorry." *Get a grip.* As the siren faded she settled back into the position she had been in before. Rubbing the spot he had rubbed, she asked, "Are you okay now?"

"I am now," putting his arm back around her middle and pulling her closer.

But she was not okay. She could still hear the siren—but it was not the siren outside. It was the ambulance coming for Marissa while Nattie held her in her arms.

The sound of the siren was getting closer, but it was not drowning out the sound of Marissa struggling to breathe. Marissa had allowed Nattie to cradle her, lifting her shoulders and head up off the sidewalk, bending her in the middle slightly. The position seemed to make it easier for her to breathe. She tried to speak, but could not.

Putting her right index finger gently on Marissa's lips, Nattie whispered, "It's okay. The ambulance is on the way. Just rest. Be still."

The color and pattern of the scarf she held against the wound were unrecognizable when she checked it. At least she was holding the right place. She would not look there again. "Hurry," she silently told the ambulance. Then she stole a glance at Marissa's eyes. She had been avoiding Marissa's eyes—the eyes that so intrigued her earlier.

Marissa was just watching her. Just watching. She did not look like anything Nattie had expected when she had not looked. No pain. No fear. No confusion. Her eyes were pensive, like watching Nattie was the most fascinating thing she had ever seen. Nattie bent forward, moving closer, but Marissa's eyes did not follow her own.

Marissa was not watching her. She opened her lips to speak, but no sound came forth.

Leaning forward and turning her head, Nattie placed her ear next to Marissa's mouth. What she heard was muffled, and it would take her a good while to unscramble it in her mind. Without flinch or sound Marissa's body went limp in Nattie's arms. Frantically Nattie looked into Marissa's eyes and confirmed what she already knew.

As Nattie remembered those eyes, she stared at the fire and tried, unsuccessfully, to control her breathing. She could not imagine ever forgetting that look. Then, in an instant, it became clear what Marissa had said.

"There are angels watching."

Names of People In
Why Bristol?

Abraham "Ozzie" Applewhite Member of the Dog Pack

Amanda Darnell White* From Nattie's Yoga class; works at Bristol Motor Speedway(BMS)

Angie Simmons Taylor the daughter of Ike & Michelle Simmons

Arnond Lanesse** Chef at The Burger Bar, downtown Bristol, VA

Asoph Saylor Author, this character first appears in WHY ME?

Beau Robinette Chef at Our House Tavern; this character first appears in WHY HIM? the 2nd WHY? novel

Bruton Smith** promoter and owner/CEO of NASCAR track owner Speedway Motorsports, Inc

Cami Timmons Armbrust* Public Relations for BMS

Carol Watson* Bubbly worker at Manna Bagel

Charlotte Jamison Local marriage counselor/psychotherapist

Corey Henson* Young man working at the Grind House, coffee shop in downtown Bristol

Debbie Duncan Standing Monday morning breakfast appointment with Nattie

Dick Goldman Member of the Dog Pack—2nd to be murdered

Dog Pack Group of vendors that work together traveling from event to event; first met serving together in Viet Nam

Elaine Claire Prostitute

Elijah Gorzilanski Samantha's husband

Eli Anderson Teenage boy befriended by Nattie; loves to bake and often left goodies for Nattie in WHY ME? the 3rd WHY? novel

Emma Iverson Public Relations Director at BMS

Grey Troutman Member of the Dog Pack

Hank Williams** Famous Country and Western singer from the 1940's

Herman Ellis Member of the Dog Pack; 1st to be murdered

Hiram Morland Detective Agency Where Nattie began P.I .career as receptionist

Ike Simmons Member of the Dog Pack; Corporal in Viet Nam, kept a detailed journal

Ingrid O'Brien Mother of Nattie and Kevin; married to Lionel (attorney)

Jackie Ke* Head of Detective Agency in Oklahoma

Joe Tennis** Reporter from Bristol Herald Currier who wrote an article about Hank Williams for The Burger Bar

John Early Police officer—Bristol PD;

Justin "Dok" Doktor* Part of the Dog Pack in Viet Nam; currently EMT in Indian Trail, North Carolina

Kent Paulette* Part of the Dog Pack in Viet Nam; now an artist living in North Carolina

Kevin Johnson Office manager of Detective Agency and brother of Nattie

Kristen Bell** American Actress; recently in the TV detective series Veronica Mars

Lawrence "Larry" Troutman Member of the Dog Pack

Lionel O'Brien Stepfather to Nattie and Kevin; Ingrid's 2nd husband

Louis Dobbs Original leader of the Dog Pack—sergeant in Viet Nam

Lucas "Junior" Dobbs Louis's son; replaced Ike Simmons as member of the Dog Pack

Mac McElroy* General manager of BMS

Maggie Lawson* 2009 Miss Virginia Teen USA

Margie worker at Manna Bagel

Marissa Ferguson Lead detective—Bristol PD

Megan Jean Musician

Michael Wade* member of the Dog Pack in Viet Nam; retired Fighter, now teaching school in Lexington, KY

Michelle Williams** Former women's basketball coach at King College

Michelle "Mike" Simmons Ike Simmons' wife; nicknamed Mike from Mike & Ike's Candy

Natasha McMorales Nattie's Private Investigator Agency name

Nathan Morland Nattie's ex-husband; Hiram Morland's sister's son

Nattie Moreland Owner/operator of the Natasha McMorales Detective Agency

Pam Zalewski* BMS receptionist

Reed "Red" Hill Nicknamed "Red" because of his red hair; member of the Dog Pack; Sunny Hill's uncle

Robert "Bobby" Dobbs Louis Dobb's 2nd son—he took his father's spot in the Dog Pack

Robin Bailey* Waitress at The Grind House coffee shop in downtown Bristol, VA

Roscoe "Sorceo" Phillips* Member of the Dog Pack in Viet Nam; now goes by "Sorceo" and teaches in Lexington, KY

Samantha Gorzilanski Lionel's daughter from first marriage

Shelley Waitress at Burger Bar (downtown Bristol)

Song Lee Goldman Vietnamese woman; Dick Goldman's widow

Stan Berringer** Beer conesseuer at Inari Wine Shop, in downtown Bristol

Steve Hawkins** Spokesperson on WXBQ & hosts morning show

Sunny Hill niece of "Red" Hill—she took her Uncle's spot in the Dog Pack when he went to prison

Trevor Gorzilanski Samantha & Elijah's son

* These are names of real people who thought it would be fun to be named in a novel. In all cases their name was used in a fictitious manner and with their approval.

** These are real people referred to as they really are.

For other titles, authors blog, photos,
and discount codes:

www.csthompsonbooks.com

Other titles in the WHY MYSTERY series:

Why Natasha?

Why Him?

Why Me?

www.ingramcontent.com/pod-product-compliance
Lightning Source LLC
Chambersburg PA
CBHW060927120626
46557CB00003B/908